Motes Played

# Motes Played

A Post-Self story

*A LITTLE BOOK FOR LITTLE SKUNKS*

Madison Rye Progress
and Samantha Yule Fireheart

ISBN: 978-1-948743-45-7

*Motes Played*



This book uses the fonts Gentium Book Basic, ROCK SALT, Gotu and Linux Biolinum O and was typeset with X⅃LATEX.

# Post-Self books

The Post-Self Cycle
by Madison Rye Progress (as Madison Scott-Clary)

I. *Qoheleth*
II. *Toledot*
III. *Nevi'im*
IV. *Mitzvot*

*Clade — A Post-Self Anthology*
Various authors

*Unintended Tendencies*
by JL Conway

*Marsh*
by Madison Rye Progress *et al.*

*Motes Played*
by Madison Rye Progress & Samantha Yule Fireheart

*Ask. — An Odist Q&A*
Various authors

*Idumea*
Madison Rye Progress *et al.*

Learn more at *post-self.ink*

**Note:** this book relies on the plots of The Post-Self Cycle, particularly *Mitzvot*. It is strongly recommended that you read those
works first. They may all be found *post-self.ink/cycle* as paper-
backs, ebooks, and free to read in the browser. If you would prefer to jump right in, spoilers be damned, you can find a primer
in the appendices on page 209 to get you started.

The tilde (~) is the punctuation mark of whimsy and on this
I will not be swayed.


**Content notes:** Contains mentions of rough, but consensual sex
with one vague description; blood; adult characters engaging
with the world as children, unrelated to sex; themes of familial
abuse.

*To The Lament, who offered me reclamation.*
*—Madison Rye Progress*

# Motes Played

She died at play,
Gamboled away
Her lease of spotted hours,
Then sank as gaily as a Turk
Upon a Couch of flowers.

Her ghost strolled softly o'er the hill
Yesterday, and Today,
Her vestments as the silver fleece —
Her countenance as spray.

— *Emily Dickinson*

Motes — 2362

# 1

Motes played.

She played in color. She played in paint. She painted the backdrops for the productions. She painted the props that sat on the stage or rested in the actors' hands. She painted the stage itself, the matte black of so many past productions long abandoned. She painted her nails, her claws, herself. She got it on her fur. She got it on her clothes. She got stripes over her ears and polka-dots on her nose. She painted her dreams, those serene and idyllic landscapes interrupted by hyperblack squares, unexpected and unexplained holes in the world that depicted a nothing-ness, a missing-ness, a not-there-ness that slid easily between the border of absurd and unnerving. She painted the holes in the world that she dreamed about but was afraid to touch and yet which would not stop touching her mind in turn.

She played in her free time, such as it was—after all, her work, such as it was, was a joy beyond joys, but everything is a sometimes food. She played hide-and-seek in the auditorium. She played tag with the performers and techs. She played pretend. She played horses and kitties and mousies. She played with Warmth In Fire, endless forks dotting countless landscapes, leapfrogging over each other across fields and between trees, bouncing off the walls of canyons and cities, colliding with force enough to knock them spinning and send them dizzy. She hunted down her friends and played hide-and-seek, yes, and tag and horses and kitties and mousies. She hunted down her friends and played puzzle games and rhythm games and stealth games and real life platformers and turn-based sims that locked her in place when it was not her turn.

She played with her form. She played with her fur. She played with her mane. She played with her claws and with her tail. She played with her size. She played with her age. She played when she presented as twenty. She played when she presented as twelve. She played when she presented as five. She played always, even when she was as old as the rest of her clade—what was it, now? 275? 276?

She played with life, enjoying and enjoying and enjoying.

She played with death. She had died countless times, onstage and off—to knives, to falls, to drowning, to games, to those who said they loved her, to those who said they hated her.

She played with identity. She played with fire.

Motes played because she was a kid and she was a kid because she played. She was a kid because kids are resilient. She was a kid because kids bounced, because they fell, cried, and then picked themselves up once more and went back to playing. She was a kid because she liked being small. She was a kid because she liked it when others played, too. She liked when others fell into enjoyment and laughter along with her. She liked the way that it brought out the best in those in her life. She was a kid because a life would not truly be complete without kids, and she believed with all of her heart that life should be complete.

She played because she *was* play. Play incarnate.

And so Motes played.

She sat atop her stool, one of her feet perched up there with her so that she could rest her chin somewhere while she painted. A palette sat on an infinitely positionable nothing beside her. A canvas sat on an easel, rickety and well-loved, before her. A brush sat in her paw, and paint sat on the brush. A thin, black rectangle sat on that canvas, as did a mountainous landscape. Music sat in her ears, chirpy and glitchy to offset the serenity of the scene in a new way.

She hummed. She sang. Her tail fwipped this way, flopped that in time with the music. She painted and painted and painted until the painting was finished—there was no guarantee of when that would be: the painting would be done when it was done, as it now was—and when it was finished, she stopped.

Slipping off her stool, she stumbled clumsily to the side, laughing at the sudden rush of pins-and-needles to her backside and the base of her tail. She inserted a step in her list of things to do before cleaning and plopped down onto her belly, using the remainder of the ochre paint in the brush to doodle the face of a fennec fox on the hardboard floor of her studio. It was one of thousands by now, and they had long since started to overlap.

Once feeling returned to her rump, she pushed herself back to sit cross-legged and started the process of actually cleaning up.

She used to just wave away her supplies, either letting them dissipate back into her memories or float back to their proper locations in her studio, but some decades prior, she had started using the process of putting things away by hand to unwind from the context of painting.

She split the difference today and forked quickly into four Moteses: one hauled the stool up above her head and trundled over to plop it down in the corner by the workbench; one ran off with the brush and palette to wash them off in the sink; one brought the easel, painting still clamped to it, over to the corner to dry; one tried to do a handstand in the middle of the room while Motes#Root watched. Eventually, she managed for a few seconds before collapsing into a giggling heap.

One by one, the various Moteses quit until #Root was the

only one remaining. She pushed herself to her feet, stretched, and padded out of the pleasantly cluttered studio.

"Lights, Dot."

Motes jumped at the sound of A Finger Pointing's voice from the couch beside the door. "Oh! Yeah!" she said, forking off one more ephemeral instance to go flip the switch in the studio, make some spooky noises, then quit, all while #Root climbed up to join her down-tree instance on the couch, slouching against her side.

"All done painting?" Beholden asked, the other, larger skunk not yet looking up from where she was slicing a lime into wedges at the bar.

"Mmhm."

A Finger Pointing ruffled a hand lazily through the skunk's mane. "What were you working on, my dear?"

"Same sort of thing," she said, squinting her eyes shut lest they be poked by errant strands of that longer fur. "The shapes in my dreams are getting narrower and flatter, now."

"Are you going to wind up painting thin black lines in another hundred years?" Beholden asked from the bar, a grin audible in her voice. "Just a beautiful landscape cut in half by a hair?"

Motes giggled. "I do not know. Probably. Are you making drinks, Bee?"

The other skunk scoffed, tossing her head back, adopting a scolding tone. "Am I making drinks? Am *I* making drinks? And We Are The Motes In The Stage-Lights, what happened to your brain?" She laughed, adding, "Why? Want one too?"

Motes blew a raspberry in response. "Yes please!"

"Beholden To The Heat Of The Lamps of the Ode clade, you had best not be feeding the child gin," A Finger Pointing scolded in turn, leaning hard into that full name. Her scowl was nevertheless patently overwrought.

"Right, virgin gin fizz it is."

"*Maaa~*" Motes whined. "I am a grown up!"

"You are seven, my dear," A Finger Pointing retorted.

Another raspberry.

Beholden poured a tall gin fizz to share with herself and her partner-*cum*-cocladist, lime muddled with sugar and cardamom bitters, gin and soda water. Then she made a second glass sans alcohol and turned to lean back against the edge of the bar, drink in one paw and bottle of gin in the other, finally facing the two cuddled up on the couch. She 'absentmindedly' started to top up the glass from the bottle. "Oh, *right!* You said virgin," she said, mock surprise in her voice. Alcohol continued to pour. She winked to the skunklet. "Oh no. *Oh no!* That is *way* too much! Motes! You had better not drink this!"

They all laughed.

Beholden padded over to join them on the couch. She took a long sip from one of the glasses before passing it over to A Finger Pointing, handing the other over to Motes. "We are headed out to a pub tonight with a few others, kiddo. Jazz and burgers and too much whiskey."

"Is that why you are all dressed up?" Motes asked, her paint-spattered overalls contrasting with both of their all-black ensembles.

They both nodded.

"Who will be there?"

"Ioan, May Then My Name, Unbidden, Ray and Loam..." Beholden said, ticking off names on her fingers. "The usual crowd."

"Can I come?"

A Finger Pointing shrugged. "I do not see why not. Do you want to?"

Motes grinned. "Not really. I just wanted to see if I could."

Her down-tree pinched her ear between her fingers. "Very well. Will you be staying here by yourself, then?"

She laughed, tilting her head and taking a lapping sip of her drink. "Maybe. Maybe I will find someone to flop with."

"Cuddly Dot?" Beholden asked, leaning closer to sandwich her between her two guardians, between Ma and Bee.

Motes wriggled right in between them. "Mmhm. Not tired, just lazy."

"Flop away," A Finger Pointing said fondly. "Who do you think you will ask?"

She shrugged. "Beckoning and Muse? Slow Hours, maybe? Dry Grass? I think Warmth is feeling a bit fussy."

"Two peas in a pod," Beholden said. "Two little fusspots."

"Am not!"

"No, no. Beholden is right. You are absolutely a fusspot," A Finger Pointing said. "Why is Warmth In Fire feeling fussy?"

"I do not know. Usually that happens when ey gets a letter from one of the Dear-cules."

"Mm, usually Pollux, yes." She sighed, passing the drink back to Beholden and resting her head against the back of the couch. "It has been a while since you bothered Dry Grass, then. You flopped on Slow Hours earlier today and pestered your aunts earlier this week. You tracked soil all over the floor, remember?"

"Alright, I will ping her soon, then."

"Good girl."

"Going to make her cook you something ridiculous?" Beholden asked. "Nuggets and fries and mac and cheese?"

"Of course," Motes said, nose poking haughtily up into the air. "Not a single green thing on the plate."

"Right." The other skunk laughed. "You know, I am always surprised by how much our tastes have diverged since we were forked. Here I am, the bitter housewife to boss's sourness–"

"Not your boss," A Finger Pointing said lazily.

"Fine, to *Time* Is A Finger *Pointing* At *Itself's* sourness."

This netted her a tug on the ear, which earned a laugh in turn.

She poked Motes in the belly. "Here you are, fat little skunk–"

Motes snorted. "You are also a fat skunk, though."

"Complaining? I thought not. You have fallen asleep on my belly more than once this week. Here you are talking about a plate of salt and carbs while I am looking forward to a salad the size of my head and a burger that is also mostly salad."

"I *also* like those things, though," Motes countered. "Like, I would eat the heck out of a salad right about now."

"You just have a bit to commit to," A Finger Pointing said, nodding. "And we are nothing if not ourselves when it comes to committing to a bit."

"Exactly! We are the same age, right? We were the same person until we were 41, right? I have just had, like...two hundred years to pick my own bit to commit to. I am the kid, you are the weirdo who makes really crazy music, Ma is the one who does all the schmoozing and stuff."

"*Schmoozing,* huh?" A Finger Pointing laughed. "I suppose that is as good a way to put it as any. Someone has to keep this band of layabouts moving. Someone has to grease all the squeaky wheels in the clade."

"There are more than a few of those," Beholden said from behind her drink.

"We are all allowed to be squeaky wheels now and then, and that includes you, my muse."

"I would trust no one else to get me all greased up," the skunk said, leering.

"You think you are so slick, Beholden, but you *had* to have gotten that from somewhere."

The playful banter continued, and while she would occasionally poke her snout in to make a quip of her own, Motes largely just savored her drink, bitter and sour and sweet, and the comfort of being nestled in between her two cocladists, thinking.

She thought about the more than two centuries that had passed since A Finger Pointing had forked into the other nine instances of her stanza, that point when Motes had become Motes. She thought about the time that had followed when she remained essentially the version of A Finger Pointing who had taken up responsibility for sets and props, about those slow years of individuation and differentiation. She thought about the way she had started to toy with her appearance, her actions, her approach to life, and how she had steered herself into this focus on play to reclaim a childhood that had, yes, been pleasant enough, and yet which could have been so much *more,* now that she had all the time in the world. Something to live intentionally. Something to savor.

It had not always been smooth, to be sure. The compromises she made early on far outnumbered the ways in which she was earnest to herself.

She did not blame A Finger Pointing for suggesting such compromises, never once. She, of all those in her life, was trustworthy. Motes had once *been* her, after all, yes? They had had their spats—more than a few—as would be the case between any parent and child—as would be the case between any two individuals. She had had spats with more than just Ma. She and Beholden had fought, and at times bitterly, and it was at those times that Bee's guardianship had felt most precarious. It had never disappeared, but it had verged well into the realm of sister—the realm of Slow Hours—or bestest friend — that of of Warmth In Fire—and away from guardian, away from that parental love.

She did not remember what the spats were about. She could, yes, her memory was as imperfectible as anyone else's on the three Systems. But she would not, because that was not the point. The point was that she was Motes. She was their Dot, their *dóttir.* She was the kid, and they were the grown-ups who loved her.

And so their protectiveness made sense, yes? They wanted to keep her safe, yes? They just could not help but keep *themselves* safe as well, yes?

And that is where the friction came from. It came from others fussing about Motes-as-kid.

She was not always. Often, she was in her early twenties. Certainly a far cry from the 41 she had been when she had been forked, or the 31 she had been when Michelle Hadje had first uploaded, but still, far more acceptable in the eyes of many on the System, far more acceptable in the eyes of the rest of the Ode clade.

It was them, through A Finger Pointing and, on a few occasions, through Slow Hours and Time Rushes, who suggested that she should not do this thing. It was too close, they said, to unwelcome paraphilias, here on the System where one had to be at least eighteen to upload. It was too close, they said, to coming off as someone seeking unwanted attention, affection, sexuality. "I understand that you wish to reclaim childhood," they told her through her ma or siblings. "But you must understand the optics." Never mind that she had long since set aside sexuality while in this form, that she harbored her own fears of those offering unwanted attention, affection, sex. No, it was the *optics* that needed minding.

And so she kept it under wraps for years and decades.

First it was the feelings she kept to herself. She alone knew them, and then her stanza alone knew them, but no one else.

Then, it was the appearance that she kept to herself. While, shortly after happening on these feelings, she had built herself into an image of youth parked squarely in her early twenties, a human who dressed in flower-embroidered jeans and blouses, who so often wore a flower crown in her hair, who embodied flower-child, she now spent weeks and months tuning various aspects of her shape, of her sensorium. A skunk like so many of her cocladists, rather than a human. Shorter, yes, but that is not all that makes a child. Shorter, proportionately different, clumsier, less developed in all ways aside from mental acuity. Just a kid.

She alone knew this shape, alone in her room, alone in her apartment, alone in her studio with the doors securely shut and the premises swept. She alone knew what she looked like, and then her stanza knew, but precious few others.

When first she began to explore outside the sphere of her stanza, when she first began to be perceived by the world around her, she lasted perhaps a week before the first gentle suggestions began to arrive. Perhaps this was just an 'us' thing, yes? A thing for playing with just Au Lieu Du Rêve, our little theatre troupe? We can play with these feelings somewhere safe.

The discussion of optics did not show up for another few years as she tested the limits of this admonition. More people had uploaded, after all. More furries, yes, and more people with similar interests. There were more friends to be made.

And yet she was of the Ode, was she not? There was an image to maintain that extended beyond the individual.

The feelings, the appearance, rinse and repeat with this and that, with moving in together, with the familial language of 'Ma' and 'Sis', with sharing a bed when she had a nightmare, as any Odist might. Again and again pushing gently at limitations to search for a slow form of change.

Still, she did as she was told and kept this particular sense of family to herself and those she loved. She was a good girl, of course, always tried to be, but she was also as much an Odist as those who spoke so often of optics. She saw the trends, the prickly taboo against intraclade relationships like that of A Finger Pointing and Beholden, how the subversiveness of found family might rub up against that. She had her guesses, but–

"Motes? Did you hear what I said?" Beholden asked, ruffling her mane all up.

"Nope~" Motes said, smiling primly. "I have been ignoring you both."

Beholden rolled her eyes. "Brat. Lost in thought?"

She shrugged, sipping her drink yet more. "I guess. Was thinking of fusspots and all the trouble calling Ma 'Ma' caused. Glad it is not a thing anymore."

"*Less* of a thing," A Finger Pointing corrected. "It is not *not* a thing. What Beholden was saying, though, is that we were going to head off. The offer stands for you to join us, Dot."

Motes let the thought go as the topic was deftly changed. "Nah, it is okay, I will stay here and see if Dry Grass wants to flop."

"Flop and draw?"

"Or paint nails or chat or whatever. There is lots we can do."

With their final goodbyes and myriad kisses, Motes was left alone once more.

She cued up more music, quieter this time, then padded to the kitchen and started a sensorium message.

*"Dry Grass Dry Grass Dry Grass!"*

There was a moment's silence, a sense of laughter, and then, *"Motes Motes Motes! How are you, skunklet?"*

*"Booored. Ma and Bee left to go to a pub or something with May and Ioan, and I felt like flopping instead,"* she sent as she dug through the fridge—more a front-end to the exchange than anything. *"They suggested I see if you were free if I got lonely."*

*"And here you are, pinging me, yes."*

"*Mmhm. Was going to make a food or two. Do you want some?*"

There was a sensation of a haughty frown from Dry Grass. "*Are you allowed to be using the stove, young miss?*"

Motes sighed dramatically. "*Fiiine, I will fork older.*"

"*Good girl,*" came the response. "*I have seen you catch yourself on fire before, and am not keen on a repeat of that.*"

"*That was one time!*"

"*I am told you are into a double digit number of times, Motes.*"

Motes snorted, pulled out frozen fries and nuggets from the exchange, as well as some macaroni and cheese—the good kind, baked in a casserole with crispy panko on top; she still had taste, after all. "*I am making fries and nuggets and maccy-chee,*" she sent. On a whim, she also pulled out lettuce, cherry tomatoes, and radishes. "*And a salad the size of my head.*"

Dry Grass laughed. "*You had me at maccy-chee. Shall I come over now?*"

"*Yes, please!*"

No sooner had the message completed than Dry Grass blinked into being on the default arrival point over by the front door.

Motes finished shoving the tray of salad ingredients up onto the counter and zipped over to her cross-tree cocladist, all but launching herself into her arms. Dry Grass caught her, letting her momentum swing both human and skunk around in a circle. "Hey, little one! Way to go almost knocking me over."

"I am not sorry!" Motes said and just as quickly dashed away and back to the kitchen. "Help me cut up everything. I am going to nick a claw, I know it."

Dry Grass followed after more sedately. "Of course. Would not want you losing a finger."

"I have *never* done that one," Motes said, dragging a chair over to the counter to stand on. "I mostly just need help with the tomatoes. They always go flying. Oh! And can you turn on the oven?"

By their powers combined, the two Odists managed to pull together a meal, exactly as Motes had described it. The salad turned out to be the breakaway winner of the bunch. Fries and nuggets are known quantities, but where the macaroni and cheese bake was good, something about the refreshing salad, the tang of the dressing, the satisfying pop of the tomatoes (many of which they wound up leaving whole) managed to hit the spot in a way none of the other dishes did.

Once the dishes had been waved away and drinks had been made—sweeter cocktails that once more got her a good-natured ribbing—Motes summoned up some simple tatami mats for them to lay on on the floor, side cozied up against side, while she painted her claws and Dry Grass's nails with a fine-tipped brush, little spirals and curlicues in pink and yellow.

"What is on your mind, kiddo?" Dry Grass asked. "Usually you do not want to just flop unless you are already worn out or something got you all thinky."

"I dunno," she said. The use of a contraction itched, brushing against the linguistic idiosyncrasies that plagued all of the Odists, even these many years later, but she had practiced for certain occasions. She shrugged, careful not to mess up the current shape. "I spent the day with Slow Hours and Sasha, and they got to talking about the past because Sasha had a question for

Slowers. Just thinking about being me."

" 'Being you'?"

"Uh huh, like the whole kidcore thing. I was thinking about how upset it made people for a long time. Even me. I would hear a thing and get all huffy for a while and go Big Motes for a month or two." She giggled, shrugged. "It all seems really silly now, but it stuck with me."

Dry Grass hummed thoughtfully. "Well, I am glad that it has gotten to the point of being silly. Are you thinking about the clade stuff?"

"A little, yeah," she hazarded, finishing up the last of Dry Grass's nails. "I was thinking about the whole optics thing, which I thought was all the eighth stanza at first, but I guess it came from all over."

"It did, yes. Most of it came from my stanza, actually."

Motes tilted her head, squinting at her.

Holding up her hands disarmingly, Dry Grass added quickly, "Not from me, my dear. Never from me. Most all of it came from Hammered Silver. A lot of her up-trees did not particularly care, and you know I actively like it."

The skunk's smile returned. "I know. You are nice to me. I had figured if not the eighth, then In Dreams would have been the one."

"Oh, she was definitely another one of the big culprits, at least early on. Do not get me wrong, I like the seventh stanza alright, but In Dreams can be a stickler over...well, most anything, really."

"Yeah, she pulled me aside once and started talking about there being a time and a place and blah blah blah."

"There is something to be said for curating one's experiences, but anyone who says the words 'there is a time and a place for everything' is just being a bitch. Pardon my language."

"What was Hammered Silver's problem, then?"

Dry Grass frowned, looking down at her spread out fingers, watching the polish dry. "It is hard to put succinctly into words that make sense because then it just comes off as a series of tautologies. She thinks that there are children and there are adults. She thinks this because that is what makes a mother a mother to someone. The child is the child and the adult is the adult in contrast. They are complements. It is all very prescriptive."

Motes frowned and pulled apart the logic, doodling pink spirals onto her fingerpads. "So she thinks kids have to be actually kids? *Actual* children, even if there are none here? You still have to be over eighteen to upload."

"I think so, yes, though it does not help that you are a co-cladist of hers."

"Is this that stupid optics thing again?"

"I do not know. Certainly in part, though it is also in part because, if you are her, then you could not be her child. It is another form of an intraclade relationship." She hesitated, then added, "It means that she has the capability to become like you, yes? That all of us have that within us, yes?"

"Oh god," Motes said, laughing. "I cannot imagine Hammered Silver as a kid. She would be one of those prissy, stuck up girls who is the daughter of the PTA president or something."

Dry Grass laughed as well. "She is already essentially the prissy HOA president. I respect her as a person, but I do not like her, and I *certainly* do not respect her authority."

"Right, because she wants you to not talk to *any* of us."

She nodded. "She cut off the first, eighth, and part of the ninth stanzas, but also the entire fifth stanza since you still talked with Sasha."

Motes groaned and rolled onto her back, holding her paws up in the air to inspect her claws. "Which is stupid, because Sasha is nice."

"She really is, though I have not had as much a chance to speak with her as I might like. She was the last straw in a whole series of events. She does not like Sasha, does not like you, she *really* does not like the family dynamic you have set up."

Bristling, Motes glared down at the polish and brush. "It is all well and good that she not like me, but to not like my family is bullcrap."

Dry Grass nodded, expression serious. "It absolutely is. She has gotten quite upset about it a few times, but I just smile and nod and tune her out when she goes into her self-righteous spirals. I am not the type to cut anyone out of my life, for better or worse, but I will absolutely ignore people."

Motes huffed, nodded. "Good. If you stop talking to me, I *will* cry."

"Perish the thought!" Dry Grass laughed and leaned over to hug her cocladist, careful of her nails. "I will not. Do not worry, my dear, you are stuck with me for a good while yet. I would rather tell Hammered Silver to go fuck herself."

2

Motes played.

Tonight, she played hard. It was a Big Motes night. It was a human night. It was a grown up night. It was a night for hovering somewhere between twenty and twenty-five. It was a night for standing as tall as Beholden, as tall as so many of the other Odists, yet far more lithe. Tonight, she dressed up in her finest crepe-cotton blouse and gauzy skirt, and she braided for herself a fresh crown of flowers—marigolds, this time—grown by Beckoning and Muse, A Finger Pointing and Beholden's long-lived up-tree instances A Finger Curled and Beholden To The Music Of The Spheres.

Tonight, Motes played in hedonism. A night at a restaurant out on the town, where she stuffed herself with two Chicago-style hot dogs. "Drag them through the garden!" She laughed—and she was always laughing. "Everything but the ketchup!" A night when she ate all of her fries, and even mopped up the last of the fry sauce with a fingertip.

Tonight, she played drunk: a beer with the dogs, drinks made fizzy with champagne and sweet with floral liqueurs at a pop-up bar, then fruity drinks served in tall glasses with taller straws at the venue before the headliner started, the thump of the bass from the opener echoing up through her feet, pressing at her chest, leaving a warmth in her belly that verged on sensual. Tonight, between sets or whenever she felt like she needed a break, she would waft back to the bar and order a vodka soda or some other ridiculous drink meant more to hydrate than taste good.

Tonight, Motes played as hard as ever, letting that warmth that was building low in her belly be her guide as she latched onto a dancing partner, a solidly built mustelid of some sort—an otter? A mink?—who wound his way through the crowd in a fluid motion that was dancelike even when the music had stopped.

It was a night for letting him dance closer and closer as the sets progressed, a night for letting him press a pill to her lips and beneath her tongue. It was a night for letting him push his whiskery muzzle up beneath her chin, letting him show her just how sharp his teeth were against her throat, for pressing close enough to feel just how thoroughly he shared in her excitement.

Tonight, she let him take her home. Tonight she let him pin her to the bed, paw on her shoulder and teeth on her throat. Tonight, she let him draw blood.

And then it was a night for sitting on his balcony and talking while the waves of whatever drug he'd given her continued to roll through her in languid pulses. "It is like someone is brushing the underside of my skin with satin in the best possible way," she said, and he laughed.

They sat and talked, legs dangling through the bars of the balcony's railing over an impossibly high drop, her ears filled with the chatter of an impossible myriad of monkeys some balconies over, startled from slumber by their arrival, her eyes filled with the black and gold of an impossible city built into a cylinder. He pointed to a building in the distance down the length of the cylinder, told her how that one was filled all with gardens, all flowers like those in her hair, now crushed lopsidedly from her forgetting to remove the crown when they fucked. He pointed up to the gentle glow in the sky, golden stars made of lights from so many buildings just like this one, told her that the sun here was in a long, thin line, that it turned on slowly from one end to the other so that one could see dawn coming from down the tube, could hear birdsong come on like a wave, and then turned off in the same direction in a linear sunset. He pointed from one end of the cylinder to another, the bounding walls marked by arcane symbols in neon, and explained that nearly a quarter of a billion people called this home, then laughed as she asked, "How many do you think are fucking right now?"

They added one more to that number before they slept.

And in the morning, she woke pressed against him, limbs all wrapped together and the satiny subdermal waves of sensation still lingering. She dismissed it easily and slowly disentangled herself from the still sleeping otter-or-mink—fisher?—and started to pull stuff from the exchange for breakfast. Cold, cured meats and fish. Cold cheeses. Cold vegetables, fresh and pickled. Dense, nutty bread. Small pastries.

They sat on the balcony once more, out in the bright sun, and ate their breakfast together, talking of only the small things.

"Is this the type of thing where I get to know your name?" he asked at one point.

She leaned over to kiss his cheek and smiled dreamily. "Nope."

After breakfast: a shared shower, a few minutes of comfortable silence, a promise to never see each other again, a kiss, and one last piercing bite to the shoulder "for luck", leaving fresh stains of red on her blouse to join the ones from the night before.

With that, she stepped back to the theatre. It was early yet and there were no performances, but she hoped that there would be someone there to greet her, someone there to witness her coming home, disheveled and bloodied, rumpled with bent crown, looking pleased and sated. Play is magnified by being shared, yes, and witnessed. She wanted to be seen, marveled over or doted upon. She wanted her joy to be acknowledged.

Empty foyer.

Empty ticket booths.

Empty auditorium.

Empty stage, but for one skunk, kneeling in the center with a clipboard and script laid out before her in a neat arc, a bank of three different colored highlighters resting in her lap.

Where so many of the skunks of the clade had the stark contrast of black and white fur, hers was the warm brown of cinnamon with the pale cream of white chocolate. Where so many of the other skunks had black noses, black fur fading seamlessly before them, hers was far more pink, more easily seen twitching this way or that at some scent or another. Where so many of her family had long, poetic names, hers remained simple, a remnant of some more complicated past.

Motes traipsed down the long, shallow steps of the auditorium aisles, all but skipping in that long-running afterglow. "Sasha!"

Sasha lifted her head and squinted out into the relative darkness of the rows of seats, grinned, then sat up straighter, brow furrowing. "Motes, Jesus. What the hell happened to you?"

Hiking herself up onto the stage, undignified, she plopped down into a cross-legged sit before Sasha. "A fun night out is what. There was an otter."

"An otter did that?" Sasha asked, raising a brow.

"Sharp!" she explained, miming fangs with two fingers.

She laughed. "Right, right. I did not know you were into the slinky types," she said, leaning forward to gently probe at the side of Motes's neck and shoulder, investigating the shallow puncture wounds that had been left behind. "One of those 'looks worse than it is' things, seems like."

Motes sighed dreamily. "Yeah~"

Sasha snorted. "We are of a type, are we not, dear?"

"Mm? How do you mean?"

"A little bit of pain to spice things up."

"Or a lot.

"Yes. I believe that might well run in the clade, even if it was not exactly Michelle's thing."

Motes nodded. "I do not remember that from phys-side, no." She paused, head tilted and grin slowly growing on her face as she leaned closer. "Does that mean that you like that too?"

Sasha looked back down to her papers, picking up an already neat stack and racking it against the stage, a transparent attempt to hide a blush or hint of a smile. "It has come up once or twice, yes."

"Oooh, Sashaaaa~" Motes said, laughing. "But wait, does that come from May, True Name, or E.W.?"

She looked up once more, rolled her eyes. "Can you really picture May being into such pain?"

"Not at all. What about E.W., though?"

"Perhaps," she replied, thoughtful expression on her face. "There were some times in the past."

"True Name, then?" Motes said, sounding skeptical.

An eloquent shrug was the reply.

"Well, *huh,*" she said, grinning still. She could feel the limerence for her form starting to fade, could feel the humanity begin to itch, so she waved the topic away. She had been seen, had been witnessed; that was all she had needed. "But we can talk about that later. I need to re-skunk. I want to keep this shirt, though."

"Alright, dear. I shall look away."

Motes shimmied out of the blouse and folded it neatly on the stage before forking into her usual, smaller, soft-furred self once more. Once more, she was clothed in familiar corduroys and a bright blue t-shirt, leaving behind so flower-child a vibe. Younger, as well, back to that comfortable, comforting expression of youth. "Okay," she said once she was done, rolling around to lay on her belly and poke her snout at one of the piles of paper. "What are you working on, anyway?"

Sasha smiled, tipped her clipboard forward to let the skunk see the stage diagram. "Blocking. Planning. Memorization."

"Scheming!"

She laughed. "Well, perhaps that as well. Scheming about dinner. Scheming about coming home to Aurel. Scheming and dreaming."

Motes nodded, carefully turning one of the piles around to read a few lines from the script before setting it back in place. She kicked her legs lazily in the air above her, feeling her tail brush against them. She hummed a tuneless song. It was all part of the ritual of settling back into being a skunk—this engagement with fur, these childlike acts—in leaning intentionally back into her presented age—somewhere around twelve, today.

She was startled back to awareness by Sasha's voice. "What are you thinking about, little skunk?"

"Mm?"

"You seemed deep in thought." She smiled affectionately. "Or perhaps blissfully without."

Motes stuck her tongue out at her. "I was thinking about how I was talking with Dry Grass yester– the day before yesterday. She was telling me about Hammered Silver being a b-word."

Unexpectedly, Sasha winced, carefully setting down her clipboard with exaggerated care. "Yes. I am sorry, And We Are The Motes In The Stage-Lights," she said, voice and movements stiff, contrite. "It was never my intent to create such a schism in the clade."

Pushing herself to hands and knees, she crawled around the piles of script to kneel beside the other skunk and hug around her shoulders. "It is okay. I do not think it is on you," she said hastily. "Dry Grass said that that was just a...um, a last straw, not even the biggest thing."

"What did she say was?" Sasha asked quietly, shifting an arm around to hug Motes in turn.

"Me," she said, shrugging. "Or, well, she also hates me, but the biggest bit was that I call A Finger Pointing 'Ma', and that she is with Beholden."

After nearly a minute of silence, Sasha said, "Years back, centuries ago, Jonas started a project of making intraclade relationships taboo. It was a measured process intended to keep *something* taboo while the rest of the System settled into a comfortable non-normativity—or even queer-normativity—on most other relationship and identity fronts. It was a bit of discomfort to strive against." Another pause, and then, "Well, and because he was setting me up with May in the form of Zacharias to gain leverage."

"Gross."

"Very gross. I am glad to be quit of him, even if there are

times that I miss the work. All of that to say that Hammered Silver bought into that hook, line, and sinker. She truly believed that it is some horrible taboo to get in a relationship—romantic or familial—within one's own clade."

"But *she* is," Motes protested. "She is in a relationship with Waking World!"

Sasha snorted. "Do not let her hear you say that. She would say that she is not, that it is a partnership, it is two actors playing their parts: she, the mother; him, the father—dad jokes and all. They are roles in a long-running production." She winked conspiratorially, adding, "Though I am not sure that Waking World would agree with her. I think he very much thinks of himself as her husband, of the both of them as very much in love with each other."

Motes furrowed her brow in consternation. "She does not make any sense," she said. "She hates Ma and Bee for dating and hates me for being their daughter and all the others for being my siblings or whatever, and then she marries Waking World?"

"Perhaps her performance is so convincing that she is fooling us all. Perhaps she is simply fooling herself."

She scoffed. "Probably the second."

"Almost certainly," Sasha said, ruffling Motes's mane affectionately. "But it is fine. I have not spoken with her in more than a decade."

"I have not in more than a century," Motes said proudly. "So I win."

Sasha laughed and turned the ruffling into a noogie. "This is not a competition, Motes," she chided. "But if it were, then yes, you would win. She has cut off even A Finger Pointing."

Squeaking and laughing, the skunk sat up, pulling herself away from the knuckles grinding against her scalp. "I thought they were on better terms, though. Ma met with her once in a while, even."

"When she found out what I had done, Hammered silver cut all contact with the fifth, yes?"

"Mmhm. Did that include Pointillist?"

"Ohhh yes. I think Hammered Silver is more mad with her than any of the rest of the stanza."

"God," Motes muttered. "She really does sound like a total b-word."

"She is a lovely person, in her own way," Sasha said gently, then added, "Which is a bitch, yes."

The smaller skunk giggled helplessly, slouching down until she was able to use Sasha's thigh as a pillow. "Okay, but why does she hate Ma, though? She is, like...the nicest person in the whole world."

"She really is, at least to us, but she is also uncompromising to her very core. She stood up for herself and Beholden as a couple, she stood up for you as you are, she stood up for your dynamic as a family–" Sasha took a deep breath through gritted teeth. "And she stood up for me—she always has—for which I am endlessly appreciative, and endlessly frustrated that she should have cause to."

"So Hammered Silver is upset that Ma has principles," Motes said flatly. "Okay. Got it. Good good, good good good good. Wonderful."

She laughed. "Yes, apparently. A Finger Pointing had some tense meetings with her early on when it became clear—at least within the clade—that she and Beholden were in a relationship, but that tension became the norm when you started to poke your little snout–" She tapped at Motes's nose-tip, getting a smile and a chirp. "–out into the world, which led to a tacit agreement that they were essentially just meeting up to collect data on their respective stanzas, and then only when A Finger Pointing agreed not to talk about you."

Motes fell silent for a long minute, then two, and eventually rolled onto the other side so that she could bury her face against Sasha's side. "Well, that makes me feel like garbage," she mumbled.

"Hush, little skunk," Sasha said gently. "That is between A Finger Pointing and Hammered Silver. A Finger Pointing had to make a tactical decision: maintain contact with the clade, be the glue that binds so many of us together, keep tabs on Hammered Silver and her ilk; or tell Hammered Silver to kick rocks, she was going to talk about her Dot as much as she damn well pleased. Tactically, she chose to agree to not pass on information about you. Strategically, this gained her a better sense of the sixth stanza—and, to a lesser extent, the seventh later on."

She nodded, pressing her face all the firmer against the stage manager's belly.

"A Finger Pointing loves you, Motes, deeply and truly. Do not ever forget that. Hammered Silver can absolutely go kick rocks and go suck an egg and go eat coke and any number of other antiquated idioms. Your ma believed that even then, and when Hammered Silver requested that she not speak of you, in that moment, they ceased being friends and became instead polite adversaries."

"No, I believe that," Motes said, voice muffled against Sasha's blouse. "I do not blame her. Hammered Silver put her in a stupid position, so she did what she had to because *she* has principles."

"Right, and those principles go beyond just the three of you. She was thinking of Dry Grass, too, yes? And of Waking World and of Fogs The View and of Time Makes Prey, and of all of the other, nicer folks she has spoken to in the sixth stanza on the sly. Many have continued to shun me, which is fine, so be it, they value their relationship with Hammered Silver more than Dry Grass does, but at least they are still talking with A Finger Pointing."

"Yeah, true. And at least Dry Grass is still here."

"That she is." Sasha smiled, nudging Motes on the shoulder. "Now, come. Let us get you home, yes? Get you some food and let you crow about your exploits to anyone who will listen, yes? Show off your blouse, yes?"

"Okaaay~" She sighed dramatically and pushed herself up to her feet. "I had breakfast a bit ago, but I want pizza or a burger or something greasy."

Sasha laughed, forking another instance to take Motes by the paw, letting her down-tree continue working. "I am sorry that this topic has been nipping at your heels these last few days, little skunk. I have probably shared more than A Finger Pointing may have wished, but she and I will talk, and you will get your pizza or burger or pizza-burger and talk about things at your own pace, dear."

# 3

Motes played.

Today, she played prey. Today, she was a mouse to some fox, some owl, some cunning predator. She crept and crawled at first, prowling through the brush and between the trunks of trees. She stuck to where the pine needles made a thick carpet on the floor of this forest or, failing that, the hard domes of granite that interrupted it. Anything she could do to stay away from the scree or gravel, the occasional stands of deciduous trees with their noisier fallen leaves, the stands of blackberry canes that she knew would tug at her clothes and fur, leaving a wake of whimpers and vines whipping backward.

Today, she sought out all of the best ways to move. There were times when all fours was called for—when she climbed a slope, perhaps, or when she needed to force herself through some keyhole in the brush, or when she needed to be quiet. Those digger claws of hers helped at times and hindered others, and if the ones on her toes would clack against rock, she would crawl on her knuckles and knees.

Today, she listened hard, head constantly turning to build a better view of the sonic landscape of the world around her. She hunted for the rustle of branches, of footsteps, of breath. Today, her eyes were keen, her gaze sharp, flitting about to hunt for the slightest movement or out-of-place shadow.

And then there it was: the shadow. The one she knew had been tracking her. The one she had felt but not seen. The one whose footsteps were too quiet to be heard and yet which nonetheless trod the ground behind her.

Instinct took over, and Motes ran.

She ran straight forward, at first, for there was a clearing ahead of her and relatively little brush between it and her and although there was a tree smack in the middle of her path, there was space enough to either side of it to slip by without having to turn too sharply, without having to slow her headlong dash.

She ran straight forward and then, just before she actually reached the clearing, juked suddenly to the right.

It had to be a trap. It *had* to be a trap. She knew her pursuer. She knew it well. She knew they would have planned for this vision of a clearing. She knew—and she kicked herself for knowing too late—that she had been subtly guided this way, toward this clearing, toward this meadow of deceptively open space, of shin-high yellow-green grass and bobbing columbines.

Behind her, a growl, sharp and clear in the overbright air, confirmed her guess.

Her hunter was quick. Motes was not: she had stubby legs; she was soft; she was chubby.

Her hunter was nimble. Motes was not: it was hard to maintain a tight turning radius with all of the above working against her.

Her hunter was smart, but then, so was she. That was her

strength. That was how she would win. That was how she would *survive.*

Rebounding off a tree and wincing at a sudden spike of pain in her shoulder, she made a hard turn to the right once more and darted toward her hunter rather than away, pressing the attack—or at least aiming for surprise—rather than simply running and running.

There, a flash of fur amid the trees. A flash of fur and sudden, wild laughter.

She picked up the speed into an all out sprint. Her pursuer darted off at sharp angle and, as it did so, a brick wall spiraled into being before her, only a few feet on a side, and yet directly in her path, a few paces away. She had just enough time to fork mid-stride and let the new instance continue in her sprint while the old crashed into the wall with a thud and yelp, then quit.

"*Attaaaaack!*" she hollered.

"Oh! Oh oh oh!" came a voice from out the trees and her prey skidded to a halt, quickly reversing direction and racing toward her instead.

*A game of chicken, then,* she thought, grinning fiercely.

The two ran directly at each other, weaving slightly to make their way around the occasional tree.

It was Motes who caved first, ducking down onto paws and knees at the last second before the critter, who deftly leapfrogged over her with a Dopplered giggle.

"Gotcha!" ey cried, scampering off to the forest.

Motes galloped after her, laughing giddily.

A few more rounds of leapfrog—repeated a dozen times over with a dozen different instances—and both Motes and Warmth collapsed in the clearing in the woods, panting and laughing. They shoved at each other for a few seconds, rolling about in the grass and wildflowers before sprawling out on their backs, looking up into the cloud-dotted sky.

"You know," Warmth said reaching over to poke Motes in the belly. "If you were not such a fatty, you could probably outrun me."

"But I like being a fatty," Motes countered. "If you were not such a string bean, you...you would...uh...."

"Uh huh?" the other skunk prompted, grinning. "What would I do, my dear? Pray tell~"

Motes laughed and tore up a pawful of grass, tossing it ineffectually at her cocladist, who merely returned the gesture.

Which Offers Heat And Warmth In Fire was a skunk like her, small like her, but had wound up wiry and lithe, perpetually untameable fur stained here and there with green or yellow as if ey had been caught rolling in the grass and dandelions and run off before bothering to wash. A being of indeterminate gender and unsettled pronouns, it was her friend of friends, a superlative acquaintance that had led to a bond unbreakable.

They elbow-crawled over to drape unceremoniously over Motes's front, sighing now that it had caught eir breath. "You are a nerd," they said. "But I guess I like you all the same."

"Pff, call me a nerd," Motes scoffed, petting Warmth's fur up backwards to muss it all the more. "At least I am a cute nerd."

"You are that," the other skunk admitted. "So am I, mind. Probably cuter than you."

"Mmhm mmhm mmhm." She grinned down at Warmth. "Whatcha doin', anyway?"

It giggled and pushed its paws up over her face. "Motes Motes Motes! Look at you, all growed up, using contractions."

"Mmnf! Is 'whatcha' a contraction?"

"I do not know. Did you have to focus to say it?"

"A little," she admitted. "Sort of like 'kinda' or 'gonna'."

"Weirdo," ey stated plainly. "Do you mean what am I doing right now? Because I am using your fat belly as *literally* the worst pillow."

"You could get off of me at *literally* any time."

"Absolutely not."

Motes smirked. "No, I was asking what you are doing in general. What are you working on these days?"

"Oh!" They sat up cross-legged, letting Motes do the same. "I got a letter from both of the LVs, and–"

"Is that why you were mopey? You got one from Pollux?"

Its expression soured. "That was part of it. I do not want to talk about that, though. The day is sunny and bright and you are fun to be around and I also heard from Castor."

Motes nodded. "Tell me about that, then. I do not want mopey Warmth."

"Good," they said primly. "Because Codrin#Convergence got my last letter and started asking all the Artemisians ey could for foods that they liked to start sending me all sorts of different flavors. Ey is *such* a nerd. Ey practically sent me a tome describing all of the different ingredients they showed em and what they looked and tasted like on their own, and then how they were put together into different dishes and what *those* looked and tasted like."

"All of the Bălans are nerds," Motes said. "Did you write back to tell em that?"

"Mmhm, I accused em of going back to being a weirdo historian."

"Good!"

Ey laughed. "But! Do you want to taste a *frahabrodåt?*"

"What the frick is a *frahabrodåt?*"

As it spoke, ey dreamed up a shallow bowl. "No fucking clue! It apparently means 'fluffy tower'." This began to take shape. It seemed to be a lattice of fine bubbles in pale, sea-foam green. "I have only tried a few of the recipes ey sent, but this one at least gave me some good ideas." The foam began to congeal into a firmer structure that looked to have been shaped by some sort of fork into a square-ish tower. "I do not know if I would call it *good,* but I am guessing by a text description of something an alien showed a non-chef on a System that is not theirs." At last, the tower seemed to be complete, though over the next few seconds it was pocked with a few pips of what seemed to be some similarly pale-green fruit. "Here."

Motes leaned forward and squinted at the dish, sniffing. It smelled like precious little.

"I have not gotten around to adding the scent yet," Warmth explained. "That is one area where Codrin did not give much detail. I replied asking ███████ to help with things like that."

"Well, okay," she said, doubtful. She dreamed up a spoon and poked at the...foam? Froth? It was surprisingly sturdy, and although it wobbled, it did not fall over under the touch.

A grin was growing on the other skunk's face.

Bad sign.

Figuring there was nothing for it, she gathered up a spoonful of the fluff, complete with a few pips, said, "Onetwothree*go!*" and stuffed it into her mouth...then immediately raced to swallow it. "Mmnglhfnnf!"

Warmth bust into a fit of giggles and forked several times in quick succession, the crowd of em breaking into a wild applause, complete with standing ovation and shouts of 'Bravo! Brava! Bravissimo!', before quitting.

"It tastes like passion fruit and licking battery terminals at the same time," Motes cried, bringing into being a glass of water to rinse out her muzzle.

"I know, right?" ey said dreamily. "I hate it."

"So do I!" At least the water seemed to wash the taste away quickly. "Are the other ones better?"

"Oh, totally."

Motes dipped her fingers into the glass and flicked some of the water at Warmth. "Then why the fuc– why the frick did you give me *this* one?"

"Because you are a fatty and because it would be fun and because I knew you would be honest in your reaction," it said, preening.

"Yeah, well, I honestly hate it."

"Mmhm! But you saying 'passion fruit' was new. Rye just said it was "sour and sweet and unpleasant" and Praiseworthy would not try it at all. Now I can compare it to passion fruit and try new things."

"Rye is always too polite," Motes said, grinning. "But I like her."

It nodded. "She really is, and I love her. She is…mm," ey squinted up at the trees, hunting for words. "We are kind of like an extended family, yes? Like, you have your ma and Bee, and big sister Slow Hours, and so on, all super close, but my stanza is like a bunch of piblings and niblings. We all like each other, and we love family get-togethers, and Rye is the best at making them happen. She wants us all to be happy."

She waved away the utensil and glass of water, flopping back onto the grass once more. "That is why I like her, yeah," she said, folding her paws over her belly, pensive.

Warmth dismissed the *frahabrodåt* and stretched out on their front. "Now why did *you* get all mopey all of the sudden?"

She shrugged, peeking over at the other skunk through the blades of grass and drooping columbines. "Just family stuff on the brain."

"Precious little of that, my dear," ey said, gently rapping her atop the head while making a hollow clicking noise with its tongue. When Motes merely stuck out her tongue, their expression softened. "Sorry, Mote. Why family stuff? Why is that mope-inducing? Usually you love that. Sometimes you go on about 'Ma and Bee this' and 'Sis Hours that' and it is *lovely*."

"Slow Hours used to hate it when I called her that," Motes said, smirking, then returned her gaze to the sky. "Just been lots of thinking and talk lately about how much trouble me being small causes."

"But I am small."

"I know, but like the smallest. Like, the youngest."

Warmth huffed, indignant. "But *I* am the youngest! I am the babiest. That is my whole thing, yes? I am the most recently forked, the most recently-claimed line!"

Rolling over onto her side, Motes smiled apologetically at her friend. "I know, I am sorry. We are the little ones, right? Dry Grass even calls us that. Her little ones."

The other skunk subsided. "I know. And I think I know what you mean, too: there is a difference between 'the babiest Odist' and 'Actual Kid: Motes In The Stage-Lights', yes? Between looking small and living in little-space?"

"Mmhm. I knew it was weird and all, and a lot of people did not like it, but I am surprised to learn just how much some people hate it."

Ey furrowed their brow. "You are?" they asked dubiously. "I though you knew that, too."

She laughed, rolling onto her back again. "I know there are lots of people who hate the whole bit. I meant more like Hammered Silver cutting off our whole stanza."

"Oh."

"Yeah," Motes said. "Like, Sasha was the last straw, sure, but it was also because of all of that."

Warmth sighed, stretching their arms in front of em. "I know she has not *actually* cut me off, but she might as well have. Her and In Dreams both, with their stanzas."

"How do you mean?"

"Well, they cut off Dear, right?" it said. "And I am rather a lot of Dear. I am Dear and Rye and Praiseworthy. I am all of my down-trees. I *like* being all of my down-trees. I am proud of it." She grinned. "I think of all of those, they might like Rye okay, but they hate Dear, and I cannot imagine them being too into Praiseworthy after the *History* named her as the propagandist during Secession."

Motes frowned. "Wait, really?"

"I mean, I have not actually talked to them, but they cut off Dear for less." Ey laughed bitterly. "But again, I am also a little one, right? Even if not in the same way as you. My stanza also has our family dynamic, yes? I have dated a cocladist before, have I not? And My and I have been getting close again, too."

Motes laughed and clapped her paws.

Grinning, it continued, "Hell, Rye and Pointillist are *plenty* chummy, if you know what I mean."

She scoffed. "They just write each other letters."

"Yeah. *Sexy* letters."

"Well, okay," Motes said, still giggling. "Do you really think they have cut you off? Effectively if not actually, I mean."

"I have not talked with them, but neither have they talked with me," they said. "I think that I am one step away from being in their cross-hairs. I am over here doing my weird stuff, making things and food and such. I am not really political, I am not being sneaky or dating a Bălan or whatever, and My is off doing her own thing for now. I *am* part Dear, though, and I *am* small like you."

"Which do you think would piss them off more?"

"Fuck if I know," Warmth said cheerily.

Motes snorted. "You do not sound like you would mind too much."

Ey shrugged. "It would suck, but yeah." It thought for a moment, then shrugged again. "I will amend that somewhat. Even if it would not be any big loss for me, I do not think it would make any of us feel good. No one wants to be an outcast."

"Yeah..."

"Sorry, Mote." Warmth scooted closer and draped an arm over her front. "I did not mean to rub it in any."

She nodded and tugged Warmth's arm up to hug it to her front. "It is okay, just had not heard it put like that before."

"Dear got its fair share of getting cast out as it became more and more of a snotty little shit, and some of that rubbed off onto us. I have a fair few people who dislike me because of that."

"People just looking up Dear in the directory, seeing you, and then hating you for no reason?"

It grinned, nodded.

"Weeeird," Motes said, frowning.

"It is whatever. It stings sometimes, but what is there to do about it?"

"Mmhm." She sighed, finally rolling to face her cocladist. "I wonder if that is why they are so mean about all of this. The *History* came out and they felt that and realized how much it stung, so they started lashing out. I know they got mad at me before then, too, but it got way worse after that and after True Name became Sasha."

Warmth bumped eir nose against hers. "Maybe. I do not know, Mote. Even if the timing does not work, you are probably right that they feel hurt by all that. I am sorry you were also one of their targets."

She wilted, nodded. "Thanks."

"Mmhm. Now, come on, kiddo. Let us lick a battery terminal and eat a passion fruit and see how it stacks up against *frahabrodåt,* and then get some *actual* food."

# 4

Motes played.

She played on precipices. She played along the knife's edge. She played at the point of a sword, at the barrel of a gun. She played with death. She–

No.

Motes was played *with.*

She was toyed with. She was dangled by the scruff over the ledge. She was held at the point of the knife. She was backed against the wall with the barrel of a gun to her forehead. She was given a sword and told to fall on it.

Motes was played with. She was laughed at. She was belittled and torn down.

The things she loved were turned astringent and bitter. All of the play she had at the point of a knife was turned fraught with peril. All of the play with death became a threat.

All of her play, all of that work she had put into reclaiming all that had been done to her in so many lives, to turning it into a joy or a kink or simple boredom was destroyed. It was the taking of good things and turning them not into something bad, for that was simple guilt, but it was the taking of good things and turning them into something she hated, she resented, she was terrified of. All of the times that she had laughed with joy as she fell to the strike of a sword or the bullet from a gun or the point of a knife in some game or at the hands of some lover were turned to wrongnesses.

It was annihilation. It was the opposite of play—of Motes's kind of play, this reclamation of childhood. It was a negating of that play. It was a turning of joy into shame, a turning of fun into fear, a turning of laughter to ash before it leaves the mouth.

In her dream, she played a game.

She played one of those games where she forked and was rendered bodiless and immobile, while her up-tree fork was sent along a series of platforms, leaping from one to another and swiping out at skeletons and liches with a long spear. The version of her doing the attacking had an incomplete view of the world, while the disembodied Motes watched from some distance away, treating the game like a literal platformer, sending instructions to her 'character' via sensorium messages.

She knew this game. Not from having actually played it in the waking world—who knew how real it was?—but she knew this game in her dream. She breezed through levels, one after the other. Enemies fell to her spear, bosses toppled easily, and when they hit the ground, vines would sprout up and flower with a luscious scent.

She could beat this game. She knew this game. She was speed-running it. Little tricks that the game's designer had built in allowed her to skip out of the bounds of the world if she jumped at just the right point, or perhaps she would use a damage glitch to end a fight almost before it began.

She could beat the final boss, who was a mirror of herself.

She knew that there was a strike—despite the boss knowing all that she did, being her—that would take her down in an instant.

But when she got to the boss arena, no one was there. Not the crouching version of herself, purple-auraed and glowing-eyed. Just her, suddenly in one, suddenly unified instead of spread across two forks.

And then something behind her snagged her by the nape of the neck, bundling up her scruff in unseen fingers and hauling her off the ground. She cried out and kicked as she dangled, swinging blindly with her spear.

This was not supposed to happen.

Whatever it was that held her turned her slowly to face the way that she had come, and she came face to face with herself at last. Not herself as a little skunk, some ten years old, but her as she was when she uploaded. Her as Michelle Hadje/her as Sasha/her as that version of herself that flowed between the two forms, visions of skunk fur washing over skin/visions of fur falling away to reveal the human beneath. There was the exhaustion in her face/the agony in her face. There was the hoarseness of her voice/the hoarseness of her voice.

"To think that I had *this* in me," she croaked/she croaked, "To think that I could be *this* disgusting."

Motes dropped her spear. Her muscles went slack. Her voice was stolen. Her breath was robbed from her.

This was not supposed to happen.

"Who are you?" The apparition furrowed her brow/bared her teeth. "You cannot be me. You cannot be us. Who are you? Who is this pretender? Who is this nobody? Who is this nothing?"

Motes cried. She hung limply and cried before that long-dead version of herself.

This was not supposed to happen.

Michelle/Sasha sneered through that omnipresent exhaustion. "Some mote who styles herself Motes. Some grasper-after-fame. Some fetishist who wishes only to taint the Ode with lurid visions of youth."

Motes cried. She could do nothing but hang from Sasha's paw/Michelle's hand and cry, could do nothing but dangle in the grasp of this person who had always been so, so fond of her and cry.

In her free hand/paw, this ghost brought into being a dagger, silver-bladed, wood-hilted, ruby-pommeled. She reached out and slowly, almost tenderly, pressed it into Motes's paw. Holding her wrist, she brought that paw up so that the tip of the blade was pressed against the skunk's neck, pricking at the skin over her carotid. When she let go, Motes found her paw remained there, immobile, unresponsive to her efforts to pull it away.

"This is your kink, is it not 'Motes'? Your fetish, 'Speck'? 'Skunklet'?" Sasha/Michelle leaned forward, nearly nose to nose, whispered, "'*Dóttir*'?"

Motes sobbed. "Please..." she managed at last.

None of this was supposed to happen. None of this was right.

Michelle/Sasha straightened up and said, almost bored, "Well? Indulge, my dear."

With no recourse, Motes drove the blade into her own neck, an agonizing slowness that played itself out in a death she had experienced before, she had surely suffered in its own, consen-

sual way.

She died then, whimpering ever more weakly, blood staining her paw and arm and front in an outsized torrent, and as her panicked eyes drifted shut one last time, she awoke with a start, already sobbing.

The house was quiet, as it so often was at this time of the night, when Beholden and A Finger Pointing were either asleep or out at one of their jazzy nightclubs. All the same, she sent a gentle sensorium ping to A Finger Pointing, figuring it best to make sure that they were actually asleep rather than simply under a cone of silence in their room.

*"Dot?"* came the sleepy reply.

She carefully poked her nose into the room, turning the handle to the door as quietly as she could. "Ma?"

"Is everything alright, Motes?"

"Nightmare," she mumbled, still sniffling. "Can I sleep with you for a bit?"

"Of course, my dear," A Finger Pointing said, stifling a yawn. "I am busy hogging all the bed, anyway, so there is plenty of room."

Sighing in relief, the skunk nodded and padded into the room, closing the door behind her. She had to feel her way to the bed in the dark. The dark, which seemed to press in against her, bearing rapidly distorting memories of the dream. *To think that I could be this disgusting,* echoed in her head. *...lurid visions of youth...*

There was a part of her that strove to convince the rest that the voice in the dark was not that of A Finger Pointing—despite the lilting, everlasting humor that showed even in sleepiness—but that of Michelle/Sasha, her root instance who had ever loved her, now more than fifty years dead. *It is her waiting with a dagger,* that fraction of her promised. *It is her waiting with yet more cruel words.*

But then there was the bed, and then there was the hand holding up the covers to welcome her in, and then there were the arms envelop her, and then there was the feeling of a face— a human face—an unshifting face—her cocladist-*cum*-mother's face—pressed against the back of her neck, and then there was the clumsy addition of Beholden's paw draping over her side, her other cocladist-*cum*-mother clearly still more asleep than awake.

And then she finally was able to relax.

None of them spoke, once she was settled. Both A Finger Pointing and Beholden quickly drifted back to sleep, and although there were the occasional flashes of skunk/human face, exhausted and sneering, behind her closed eyelids, Motes soon followed.

It was not until morning came, when Beholden had slipped away for a few minutes and returned with three mugs of coffee on a tray, when all three of them sat up in bed, leaning against the headrest, tray set before them, that she told them of the dream.

"I do not remember it all that well, now," she said holding the oversized mug carefully in comparatively small paws. "But Michelle was there, and she was really upset with me. She kept saying that I was gross and a fetishist and stuff, and that she could not believe that she had this in her, and then she made me kill myself."

"Jesus, Dot," Beholden said, frowning over the rim of her mug. She reached her free arm around the skunk's shoulders and tugged her close against her side in a hug. "I am sorry to hear that. That sounds awful."

"It really does, my dear." A Finger Pointing leaned over to kiss at the tips of her ears. "And I think that it is demonstrably untrue that she did not have this in her. You exist, Motes. You are absolutely my up-tree, and I know where you got it from." She smiled. "And I am absolutely her up-tree, am I not?"

Doing her best to hold still despite the ticklishness of the kisses, Motes nodded. "I know. It was just a dream. Dreams are not real."

"Not unless you are Slow Hours," A Finger Pointing said, nodding. "And even then, there is no guarantee. But come, the details of the dream aside, how are you feeling now?"

"I guess I am feeling okay. It feels like any old nightmare." She furrowed her brow, picking words carefully. "It feels like it is something sticky that has gotten stuck in my fur and I have to carefully remove it. It sucks, and it is a lot of work, but it is just a silly thing that happens sometimes, right? Every time I remember driving the knife home, I just remind myself it was fake."

"Good," Beholden said, letting the smaller skunk slouch against her. "That is a good way to think of it."

A Finger Pointing leaned against Motes in turn—over her, in fact, to the point of resting her head on Beholden's shoulder. "I know that you will not be able to forget about it, not completely, but processing it for what it is—a dream—may well help it be less of a burden," she said. "I have gained comfort in that at times for my own dreams, waking and sleeping."

Motes huddled comfortably between the two. "But what does processing even mean? I feel like even my brain is yelling at me about all of this now," she asked, doing her best to keep a whine out of her voice. "I do not even know why it is all coming up so much lately."

Beholden laughed. "It is all your fault, my dear. The dream probably showed up *because* you have been thinking about it. Others have been talking with you about it *because* you keep bringing it up. Probably best to ask yourself what got you thinking about it in the first place, right?"

"I guess," she grumbled. "I will try and remember. It felt like it just kind of floated up into my mind a few weeks ago from out of nowhere."

"Remember, yes," A Finger Pointing said, yawning dramatically and leaning harder until she was able to push both of the skunks over onto their sides. She held up a hand as though inviting them to picture a tableau. "I remember the maps of the Holy Land," she lamented, quoting from some old production, some old classic. "Colored, they were. Very pretty! The Dead Sea was pale blue. The very look of it made me thirsty."

Both of the skunks fell into laughter, sprawled awkwardly beneath their down-tree instance on the bed. "That is where we will go, you used to say," Beholden said, keeping up the act. "That is where we will go for our honeymoon."

"We will swim! We will be happy!" Motes chimed in.

Sighing fondly, A Finger Pointing nodded. "We should have been poets."

Motes could tell what they were doing. She was as adept at this as they were. The job of an actor is to trick the audience—just for a moment!—that the story playing out before them is more real than the rest of the world, that it is the rest of their lives that is merely a play. A Finger Pointing and Beholden, Ma and Bee, were nudging her to set aside for now this dream-rotted headspace, this mopery.

She saw their gentle manipulation and loved them all the harder for it.

The rest of the morning passed in comfort and lazy chatter, but throughout, some portion of Motes was dedicated to thinking back, to remembering. Comfort and lazy chatter and remembering, then, before the three decided to split off to their own tasks—Beholden into two instances, one to work on music, one to the theatre; A Finger Pointing to some planned brunch; Motes to go for a walk, to go and talk.

The fifth stanza had begun its life in an apartment building in a cozy, artsy town. As many studios and penthouses as were required for one mind split ten ways. Life on Lagrange had progressed as ever, though, and soon the sense and sensation of being a part of the fifth had changed. It began to encompass relationships fleeting and lasting. It housed devotion, invited in friendship. It grew beyond the bounds of just this tenth of a clade to include all of Au Lieu Du Rêve, and some few decades on, the whole of the project decamped from their city-block sized apartment building.

Now, the fifth stanza—along with however many other lovers and friends, coworkers and groupies, up-trees and tracking instances—occupied a sprawling neighborhood of houses and townhomes, yards and copses of trees, and yes, even a playground. The whole neighborhood crowded against an untamed field, a prairie, a meadow laced up with deer trails and footpaths, dotted with yet more copses of trees lining a creek.

For each of those who lived there, the neighborhood was theirs in some specific way, and for Motes, it was hers to paint.

Motes had painted it all hundreds of times, of course.

She had painted the prairie, painted the neighborhood, painted those who lived there. She had chosen the colors of many of the houses—had even helped paint some by hand until it had gotten too boring. She had chalked up all of the sidewalks—Warmth had conspired with A Finger Pointing and Serene, the sim's designers, so that colored chalk lines flowered behind her automatically as she walked when she so desired—and she so desired—only to fade some hours later. One could always tell where Motes had come and gone.

Thus, when, still sleepy, she trudged out of the ranch-style home she shared with A Finger Pointing and Beholden, colored lines of flowering vines trailed after her bare paws. She guided those vines with her steps or, relishing in a secret pleasure, pretended like they were propelling her forward, pretending that she was a being of growth—that she was a seed, a being of potential—that she was a giant at the head of some toppled beanstalk.

The vines or her feet carried her down through the neighborhood at a contemplative pace, giving her time to think of the conversation she wanted to have before she actually had it. She spoke so often without thinking, letting that be a part of her nature rather than some simple flaw, that to approach something so deliberately as this set her mood from the beginning, and by the time she drifted up the set of steps to a duplex near the far end of the neighborhood, many of her doubts had been set atop well-lit pedestals, and placards beneath each labeled their names, their creators, their provenance.

No one answered the door when she knocked, so she hesitantly pressed the doorbell. This, she knew—for it was the same throughout the neighborhood—was created to send a sensorium ping to the inhabitant.

*Why am I so nervous?* one part of her wondered, and then another answered, *Perhaps because you are worried she will tell you the truth.* Another chimed in, *Is that not the goal? Perhaps–*

She was startled out of her anxious spiral by a gentle ping in return. *"Speck? What is up? I am at the ALDR library. Would you like me to cycle the door?"*

Motes nodded. *"Hi Slow Hours. Yes please."*

There was a quiet chime from the door and the letters on the nameplate faded from 'Slow Hours' to 'Au Lieu Du Rêve Library'. This done, there was a quiet click and the door swung lazily open.

Beyond, rather than the comfortable and comfortably her home that Slow Hours kept, there was a well-lit reading room, a solarium of sorts with glass that looked out over some far distant part of the selfsame prairie that the neighborhood abutted. A table, several chairs, and a small collection of far more comfortable recliners huddled in the middle, while beyond, a room of shelving stretched into dimness.

And there, already levering herself out of her chair, was Where It Watches The Slow Hours Progress. Sis Hours, her big sister. Slowers. Slow, if she was feeling particularly cheeky. Had Beholden been human or Slow Hours a skunk, they could easily have been mistaken for twins, so similar were their builds— short, soft, round of face with curly black hair framing that pale skin versus short, soft, round of face with thick white mane framing that black fur—and yet as soon as they spoke, the differences were immediately evident. Where Beholden was brash and snarky, Slow Hours was quiet and thoughtful. Where Beholden leaned into music as the lead sound tech, Slow Hours leaned into books as the lead script manager. Where Beholden was fun—really, truly, earnestly fun and a joy to be around—Slow

Hours was nice. She was the one with which one spoke about feelings. She was the one who cried with you.

Behind her, scattered among the shelves, several more instances of her cocladist were at work, peeking over whenever they thought she was not looking as though ready to do just that.

"Hi Speck," she said, smiling. "If you are calling me 'Slow Hours' then something must be up."

Motes huffed.

"You are transparent, my dear. It is a strength of yours." Slow Hours rested her hand atop the skunk's head. "Now, come. Do you want to go sit outside?"

"Yes please," she said, feeling suddenly smaller still.

She was a long time in opening up, which seemed to suit her cocladist just fine. Slow Hours summoned up a blanket and, disregarding the patio furniture that littered the concrete that ringed the solarium as well as the hard-packed dirt trail, picked her way out into the prairie. Holding two of the corners, she threw the blanket out to spread it over the shin-high grass. It seemed to float there, and for a long moment, neither of them moved. Skunk and woman observed this magic carpet in gingham hovering inches above the ground, bending blades and heads of stiff-stalked grass.

When Motes lingered on the trail, pensive, Slow Hours stepped onto the blanket and tramped dutifully around the rim of it, tamping down the grass so that they would not sink so deep. That done, she lowered herself to sit cross-legged near the center and patted her lap.

At last, the skunk sighed and stepped onto the blanket, lowering herself to all fours and crawling forward to flop down beside her cocladist, resting her head on her thigh.

"Now," Slow Hours began. "Tell me what is on your mind. Tell me your second greatest joy and your third greatest fear."

Unable to hide a smile, she replied, "You cannot just steal my weirdo questions like that, Slowers."

"Can and will."

She giggled faintly. "Well, okay. My second greatest joy is that you brought a fricking picnic blanket out here because you knew I would just get all frumpy in one of those stupid chairs, and my third greatest fear iiiis..." She trailed off for a moment, thinking. "I am afraid you are going to just tell me this is nothing."

"When have I ever been able to stop myself at "it is nothing", Speck?" Slow Hours tweaked one of the skunk's ears gently. "And if I do say that it is nothing, would that be so bad? You may have spent some time worrying, but is that not also time spent thinking through your emotions? We will still have spoken about *why* it is nothing."

Motes pawed up at her cocladist's hand on her ear. "Well, okay. That is fair. None of us ever seem to be able to shut up."

"You see? You do understand. Now. Tell me what is on your little skunk mind."

"I had a dream last night," she said, beginning slowly. "And I already talked about it with Ma and Bee, and I think I sort of understand the ways in which it is wrong. Like, we talked about the fact that it was just a dream, and that it was probably spurred by how much I have been thinking about that sort of thing anyway, and that, since I cannot tell why I started thinking about all of this stuff, what I need to do is to start thinking back and remembering what might have happened that started the thoughts before."

Slow Hours nodded quietly. "Start at the dream, then, and we will talk from there. I am sure that I will infer what you mean by 'this stuff'."

And so she did.

She delved deep into her memories and pulled out as many details as she could. The System would help her remember anything that would pass before her sensorium, that which she heard or saw, touched or tasted or said aloud, but not any of her thoughts or feelings.

Dreams, however, sat in some liminal space. They were built up of images, yes, and sounds, perhaps even pleasurable or painful touches, but the System did not quite know what to do with this onslaught of imagined input. It allowed her to remember distorted flashes of images with startling perfection, to remember the garbled words overheard without fault, and yet the distortion and garbled nature of each remained.

So vivid had her nightmare been, though, that Motes had no trouble recalling the emotions and thoughts that had pinned themselves so firmly to the dream.

She had often wondered if dreams took any time at all, if perhaps there was nothing while she slept and it was instead the act of waking up when the chaotic firings of her non-neurons from all that time she slept crashed and tumbled into some sense made by her newly-waking mind. Perhaps nothing happened while she slept but crude and natural processes, and it was hypnopompia where a cloud became a duck or a bunny.

She was not so sure now. The immediacy of the dream felt

too bound to time. Sure, the time spent playing the game was a haze of knowing how games work, of knowing what a speed-run was. That was non-time. That was all bunched up in impressions built from however many hundreds of such games she had played in her long, long life. She could not express whether or not the combat was good because it was neither good combat nor bad, it was just Combat™. It was just an idea.

She was not so sure that dreams were meaningless firings of neurons composed into some semblance of order in the process of waking as she recalled tearfully the way that Michelle had caught her up by the scruff and told her horrible things—such horrible, horrible things—and then bade her drive home the blade to end her own life.

All throughout, Slow Hours listened in silence, letting her talk while brushing her fingers slowly through the thick fur of her mane. Even after she finished speaking, while she lingered a while in tears, her cocladist simply sat with her in silence, stroking through her fur and sharing in those tears. It was a comforting silence. Thoughtful. Patient, with no need of filling.

Once her tears began to slow and she wiped at her nose with a tissue, Slow Hours leaned down to kiss her cheek. "I am sorry, Motes. You deserve better than what your sleeping mind has told you," she said gently. "It sounds as though this false vision of your past self was upset with two things: your explorations around age and your explorations around death, yes?"

Stifling some sniffles, aftershocks of the cry just ended, Motes nodded. "Yeah, though I think more the first," she said, wincing at the muffled sound of her voice through her congestion. It sounded round, somehow, wrong. "That is what I have been thinking about most, anyway, that would have led to a dream like that. The death was just the punishment."

"And you are not sure where these anxieties came from?"

She shook her head. "Nothing has really changed. I have been seeing friends the same amount, I had therapy with Miss Genet, I have not heard from anyone who got upset at me, nothing like that. It feels like it just popped into my head and now I have to live with it."

Slow Hours smiled down to her. "You know, A Finger Pointing mentioned to me that you had brought this up, actually. She says that you have been talking about it lately. Far more than usual."

"She did? Why?"

"Because she loves you and because I love you. Because we want to see you happy and we notice when you are not."

Motes pushed herself halfway up to sitting so that she could hug around Slow Hours's middle. "Love you too, Slowers," she said, then sat up the rest of the way, wiping yet more tears away. "I have been talking about it a lot, though, yeah. I talked about it with Ma and Bee, and I talked about it with Dry Grass, and also with Sasha and Warmth. Everyone talked about how some people in the clade got all upset about it."

She nodded. "I have heard mention of the sixth and seventh stanzas, yes, and I thought for some time that the eighth was also quite unhappy, but I believe Sasha when she says that they never really engaged with it specifically."

"Yeah. Dry Grass said that Hammered Silver was all sorts of upset about it, and I know In Dreams was pretty unhappy early on."

"Have you heard from any of them lately?"

Motes shook her head. "I never really talked to them, even going way back—I did not really need to—and they never talked to me either."

"Much of that was because A Finger Pointing fielded most of their interactions," Slow Hours said. "She is quite protective of you—of all of us—and if she can do something to protect us, she will."

"Sasha said something like that," she said, brow furrowed. "She said that Ma had been working behind the scenes to deal with Hammered Silver getting angry over just about everything."

"A Finger Pointing worked behind the scenes to deal with most things, Speck," Slow Hours said, voice fond. "*Still* works. Au Lieu Du Rêve is self-sustaining, so she is doing what she does best: caring for her stanza and for the clade as a whole, even the parts of it that dislike her. But come, this is not a conversation about her. This is about your dream. This is about how you feel."

"Right," Motes said, pushing that miserable sensation in her chest down once more. "I feel...I do not know. Usually, it feels like I am just living like myself, if it feels like anything at all. Sometimes it feels transgressive in a fun way, like when I get booted from a sim for being weird or I get strange looks on the street or whatever."

"And sometimes it feels transgressive in a bad way?" Slow Hours asked when Motes drifted to silence.

"Yeah. It feels like I am doing something wrong. That is what I got out of the dream. It was not just that I was doing a bad thing, but a *wrong* thing. A bad thing might be naughty, but a wrong thing is me fuc– messing up. It is me making a mistake. *Being* a mistake."

Her cocladist smiled sadly and reached out to take her paws in her hands. "I could tell you a million, billion, trillion times that you are doing as you say and just living like yourself, that you are not doing a wrong thing, that you are not a wrong person, but I do not think that is what you need to hear, is it, Speck?"

After a moment's hesitation, she shook her head. "That is something I know intellectually already."

"Do you want to hear my thoughts on the clade, then?"

Motes shrugged. "I guess."

Slow Hours nodded, letting her paws go. "I will not say "fuck 'em", much as either of us might want. You must not hyperfixate on them, but neither must you disregard them."

"Why? Do you have a prophecy for me?" Motes asked, smiling faintly. "The last time you gave me a prophecy, it was about whether I should stay friends with Alexei."

She laughed. "I remember that, yes. You were bound to run into someone who was also into kidcore stuff as Big Motes, and we were stifling you." The mirth faded to something more thoughtful. "But, yes, I have a prediction for you: the clade is not done with you, And We Are The Motes In The Stage-Lights. Even those who have cut you off have not forgotten you, and it is best that you not forget them."

The skunk frowned, rubbing her paws over her knees and toying with a rip in the denim of her overalls. "Okay," she mumbled. "Where do you get all of this, anyway?"

Slow Hours smirked, tapped at her temple with two fingers. "I have the outline of the world, do I not?"

Motes stuck out her tongue. "That is not an answer."

"Yes, my dear, it is," her cocladist said haughtily, then the smile returned. "But in reality, most of these prophecies or omens or forecasts that I am apparently known for are simply reads on the situation based on the stories that I have read—and I have read a *lot* of stories. The clade is not done with you because that is not how people work. They do not cut contact with an erstwhile friend and then never think of them again. They think of them *constantly*. The stories wherein 'no contact' holds without further enmity are vanishingly few."

She wilted, shoulders slumping. "So I might be hearing more of this, then? From Hammered Silver and so on?"

"You might. You might not." chuckling at the exasperated look on the skunk's face, Slow Hours leaned forward to brush some of her longer headfur from her face. "The key takeaway here, Speck, is not that you need fret about this constantly, but that you should not ignore these feelings. You should not simply dismiss those within the clade that cut contact as irrelevant. Even if they forever live only in some dusty closet in your mind, they will still live there."

"Yes, but what am I supposed to *do*?"

"Live, my dear. Grow." She laughed, adding quickly, "Not up, not if you do not want, but take that knowledge, take strength in the fact that you are living intentionally as you are in spite of them, and make yourself better for it. Live fiercely and let it inform your growth, just do not let it define you."

Motes nodded sullenly.

"I know that you said that you do not need to hear that you are not wrong or doing wrong things," Slow Hours said, drawing the skunk up into her lap. "But I will tell you all the same: you are not in any way a mistake. You are approaching this cognizant of the implications. You are being safe. You are leaning on support and protection. You are holding in your mind both the truth that this *is* you and that an expression of identity like this coming from an adult is fraught."

"I know," she mumbled, burying her face against her co-cladist's shoulder. "Thank you, Slowers."

"Of course, my dear. I am afraid that I did not do quite the job of comforting you that I might, but I do hope that you take that to heart. Live intentionally, and remember that we love you."

5

Motes stopped playing.

She stopped playing because, some weeks later, she was out with some friends, some of the others who had decided to give up on grown-up life now that they were here, now that they were decades old or centuries, now that they were functionally im-mortal. She stopped playing because, as she sprinted full-tilt after a handful of friends, dodging around benches and trees, see-saws and swings, a bolt of panic struck down her spine with an electric intensity and made her tumble into the gravel, made her skid through the pebbles until she crunched up against a jungle gym, left her nose, paws, and elbows bloodied. She stopped play-ing because for a long minute, she could not breathe, though whether from the adrenaline pulling her nerves taut or the pain in her snout or from the air being knocked out of her, she could not tell.

She stopped playing because, as she slowly pushed herself upright to a sitting position, tears already springing from her eyes, an envelope slid nonsensically from the air and fluttered to the ground before her. She stopped playing because her name—her full name, And We Are The Motes In The Stage-Lights of the Ode clade—was printed on the front of the envelope in a hand-

writing that was painfully familiar because it was her own. It was her own and it was A Finger Pointing's and it was Beholden's, it was Slow Hours's and Warmth's and Dry Grass's, and it was the handwriting that flowed from the hand of every Odist even after hundreds of years.

She stopped playing because she had a guess as to who this was from, and that only led to a second spike in anxiety, for while the first had been from a top-priority sensorium ping, this came from fear, from terror. She stopped playing as Alexei hollered, "Motes!" and started to run back to her. She stopped playing as she rolled to the side out of the sim and into her studio.

She stopped playing and, with a shaky paw still seeping blood from skinned pads, she opened the envelope.

She stopped playing and read:

**To:** And We Are The Motes In The Stage-Lights of the Ode clade **(EYES-ONLY)**
**From:** Memory Is A Mirror Of Hammered Silver of the Ode clade
**On:** systime 238+291

And We Are The Motes In The Stage-Lights,

I am breaking my communication embargo to write you regarding some concerns that I have on the current state of the clade, the fifth stanza, and you in particular.

As you know, the sixth and seventh stanzas, those of me and If I Am To Bathe In Dreams, have formally instituted a no-contact order with the first, eighth, and part of the ninth stanzas, as well as the entirety of the fifth stanza due to the ongoing association with the one who has named herself Sasha.

I do absolutely mean it when I say all of the fifth stanza. That is, we have not cut *just* Time Is A Finger Pointing At Itself out of our lives for her distasteful friendship, but her and all of her up-trees to however many degrees. That includes you, And We Are The Motes In The Stage-Lights.

It came to my attention some years back that I Remember The Rattle Of Dry Grass had nevertheless continued in her association with the fifth, particularly with you and with Time Is A Finger Pointing At Itself, given your unfortunate predilection. When first I noticed this, I discussed with her my feelings on the matter and made clear my request that she live up to the original agreement that there remain no contact between our stanza and yours. She, at the time, reminded me that this decision had been made unilaterally without input from the rest of the stanza, and yet agreed to uphold my request.

It has once again come to my attention that I Remember The Rattle Of Dry Grass is spending time with you and those you have styled your 'family'. She has the most infuriating habit of going on autopilot when I talk to her, simply nodding and saying 'mmhm' or 'yes, I see' throughout, and, with regards to this topic in particular, this has proven untenable. It is with great regret that she has been added to the no-contact list.

There is a very important set of reasons for this:

1. Time Is A Finger Pointing At Itself and Beholden To The Heat Of The Lamps's ongoing romantic relationship remains a thorn in the side of the Ode clade. Even as the taboo seems to be loosening—a thing that I attribute to the one who has named herself Sasha's ongoing existence—there remains the issue of the im-

age that this presents of the remaining Odists as a clade of some import.

2. Your insistence on both appearing as and acting like a child on a System where such remains transgressive both by its very nature and relation to paraphilia as well as by the fact that there simply are no children sys-side.

3. The 'family' dynamic that you live within inside the fifth stanza. Treating Time Is A Finger Pointing At Itself and Beholden To The Heat Of The Lamps as your 'mothers', as well as your other cocladists as your siblings, is beyond a mere dalliance, but a tainting of reputations outside merely your own; it is a way of dragging others into a behavior that has a very real impact on how they—and, by extension, the rest of the clade—are perceived.

4. The friendship between Time Is A Finger Pointing At Itself and the one who has named herself Sasha and her inclusion in not just the daily workings of Au Lieu Du Rêve but the social dealings of the fifth stanza. If I Am To Bathe In Dreams and I hold no jurisdiction over the fifth stanza, but we do hold control over our interactions with each other, and we have made our stance abundantly clear on the one who has named herself Sasha and how she has affected the reputation of the Ode clade.

5. The involvement of I Remember The Rattle Of

Dry Grass counter to my requests laid out for the entirety of my stanza. This goes beyond her disregard of the no-contact order and into her willing participation in the actions of the fifth stanza in general and engagement with you specifically: these no-contact orders are expected to be upheld by *both* parties. Yes, this is complicated by the individual nature of a cladist, and yet the request has been made, and plainly. For a member of a stanza to so flagrantly disregard a request and for that to be enabled by the other party leaves me feeling personally slighted.

Therefore, I am writing to reinforce the current status:

1. There is to be no contact between the fifth stanza and either the sixth or seventh stanzas.
2. There is to be no contact between the one who has named herself Sasha and either the sixth or seventh stanzas.
3. There is to be no contact between I Remember The Rattle Of Dry Grass and the rest of the sixth stanza until further notice.

You are not just playing a dangerous game, And We Are The Motes In The Stage-Lights; you are losing it. We *all* are losing it with you, too, with the risk that it places on the entirety of the Ode clade, even those

with whom you no longer speak. I will not say that
this is all on your head, but consider that three of
the five points above relate directly to you.

> When I was a child, I spoke like a child,
> I thought like a child, I reasoned like a
> child. When I became an adult, *I put an end
> to childish ways.*

— Memory Is A Mirror Of Hammered Silver of the
Ode clade

When Motes overflowed, she cut herself off from play. She
froze where she was. She went nonverbal, became all but catatonic. It would last days. She would disappear from the world
and she would stop playing, and if she stopped playing, she
would no longer be herself.

So, when Motes stopped playing that day, she promised herself that she would *not* do that. She promised herself that, as best
she could, she would do anything *but* that. She promised herself
that she would keep going because she did not want to be seen
like this. She did not want to be caught like this, with a letter in
her hand, with shame on her face, with guilt all matted in her
fur.

Instead, she stood up, committed the contents of the letter
to an exocortex, a hidden and compartmentalized part of her
memory that rendered it inaccessible until she went looking,
and then destroyed the original. There was a part of her that
wanted to rip it up, to rip it into confetti and stomp on the shred-
ded paper, to burn those shreds in a small pyre, to put the fire

out with her crying, to grind ash and tears together until she had a paint with which to spell out her anger and despair.

But no, she should not do that, either. She should not do anything so childish. She should not do childish things. When she was a child, yes, she spoke like a child and thought like a child and reasoned like a child. She acted like a child when she was a child. *Was.* She was not, was she? She was an adult, and when she had become an adult, it had come time to put an end to childish ways. She was no longer a child, she should not aim to remain or become a child, she was no longer a child, she was an adult, she should put away childish things, she was an adult, she no longer thought or reasoned like a child, she was an adult...

Her mind became a mire, a marsh, a crowded bog full of unpleasant smells and tangled reeds and matted rushes and wilting flowers and sickeningly green ferns and twisting roots and...

Her muscles clenched and bunched and tensed and pulled her down into a ball so that her feet were flat on the ground and her butt hovered some inches above and her face was buried in her arms where they crossed over her knees and in her ears was the rushing of so much blood and her vision was black and red and full of phosphenes and all she felt was the pain of her skinned paws and bloodied nose echoed in repeating waves radiating throughout her body.

"Oh, Dot," she heard above the din, Beholden's anxious and aching voice barely audible. "How long have you been here, my dear? You never came to dinner and– oh shit, are you okay, Motes?"

She felt, muffled by those waves of stinging and soreness, the pair of paws that had helped to gently unfold her now touching gingerly around her snout, blood all dried. She saw Beholden's face as though it was one she herself might bear in some thirty years, and that anxiety ratcheted up several notches. Any hope she had of staving off that overflow was now long, long gone. *I am an adult, I should put away childish things, I am an adult...*

"Whoa, whoa! Hey, come here," Beholden murmured, and Motes realized from some few feet above herself that she had started to thrash and wail. She looked down with distant concern.

She should stop that.

She watched her body slowly relax, watched her face screw up and the tears once more start to flow.

*Interesting,* she thought dispassionately. *Yet I acted like a child when I was a child. I am an adult...*

Her sense of self lagged behind—a hint of a mote of a Motes tethered to her body like a helium balloon on a string—as Beholden carefully lifted her unsouled-yet-still-living body and hoisted her up to carry her from her studio—*the lights, she left the lights on*—to her bedroom. A place of soft things. A soft mattress, a too-thick duvet, stuffed animals and yet more stuffed animals. *I should put away childish things, I am...*

Beholden set her on her feet and carefully lifted her muzzle to face her. "Motes, I know that you are overflowing, but can you fork for me, kiddo? Your nose is swollen and your paws look awful."

*I should fork away the childish things,* the her that lingered above thought. *I am an adult and the time has come to put away the childish things.*

"Do you think you can do that, Dot? You can fork into your PJs even, and we can get you into bed."

She saw a new instance come into being beside the first. Still a skunk. Still a kid. Still not putting away those childish things! Look! The cartoon dogs floating in space, glass helmets over their heads! Space puppies! She was an adult, it was time to put away...

The other, still-bloodied instance quit and Beholden smiled, carefully guiding the pajama-ed Motes up into bed. "Do you need anything, my dear?" she asked, signing the question in tandem.

*Hug,* Motes's body signed. *Hug. Alone. Dark.*

*And the toys?* this other her thought. *Tell her to get rid of the toys!*

But no, Beholden only hugged her, kissed her on top of the head, and tucked her in before turning out the light, telling her along each step of the way that she loved her.

*I am an adult...*

And then it was dark and she was alone, her body and this mere mote of a Motes who lingered up above.

Days passed out of time and time passed out of mind and mind drifted only in darkness where darkness gave no count of days. Delineations came only ever from within. She knew, for instance, that she got hungry at one point and quickly turned the sensation off. She knew that at one point she got too warm and so she commanded the room to be colder so that she could bundle up.

The only interruption of note that came from the outside was the door at one point creaking open. Motes did not know how long had passed—this life without play admitted no hours—

but she did know that it must have been night, for precious little light came in, and what light did make it into the room was Moon silver. She knew also that she was far closer to her body now, perhaps halfway there.

Even with so little light, it was plain to see A Finger Pointing's silhouette, tall and slender, and so she remained where she was.

Her down-tree instance did not wait by the door but instead crept in and closed it behind her, and Motes had to track her progress by the whisper of her slacks, the soft sound of her feet on the carpet. And then there was the shifting of the bed and the feeling of a weight settling down behind her, laying over the covers.

"I love you, Dot," she said, arm tucking up and around her.

Motes watched dispassionately as her body started to relax at the gesture, the words.

"I am sorry," A Finger Pointing continued in a whisper.

There was confusion, then, and a spike of anxiety—had she found out about the letter? Was Motes in trouble? Was there a 'but' coming, and A Finger Pointing was about to ask her to change?—but when only silence followed, Motes relaxed the rest of the way and nestled back into her cocladist's arms. She was not yet able to speak, was still without her beloved play, but comfort was comfort and love was love and here is where it was to be found.

Finally she slept, finally she dreamed.

# 6

Motes had, at one point, started to play.

That is how time's inevitable arrow works, after all, is it not? There was a time when Motes was not, when she had not yet existed, and then there was a point at which she began, and from then on, she existed. Her presence was in the world, and it was undeniable. There were witnesses. There were knock-on effects. She inescapably *was*.

And so, there was a time at which she did not play, did not surround herself with play, did not define herself by it, and then there was a point at which she began to play. It was a starting point. It was an inflection point, at which she collided with the idea of play and her trajectory was changed.

And yet, even before that, before Motes, before the System, before getting lost, Michelle had played, had she not? She had been a kid, yes? Michelle, even before getting her implants and becoming Sasha, had been five, had been six and seven and eight.

✰

Michelle played as well. She painted, too, back then.

Roly-poly Michelle Hadje, 263 years ago, sitting in kindergarten, shitty paintbrush in her hand, shitty tempera paint in a dish set before a shitty piece of off-white construction paper. She sat there in her silly little corduroy pants and silly little flower-print blouse, a silly little smile on her face, painting a robin in primary red and deep-dark black.

Silly, roly-poly Michelle Hadje in her dirt-brown corduroys splotched with a patch of red from having sat down directly in a puddle of paint. It was not a drip so easily wiped away but well and truly ground into the ridged fabric of her trousers.

"Oh! Miss Hadje! Michelle, Michelle, Michelle!" her teacher tutted. Miss Willard always looked as though she regretted that she was not able to scruff children, to lift them off the ground and give them a good shake, or perhaps to rub their noses in the messes they made like some naughty pooch. "Your mother will be so upset, won't she?"

And Michelle cried. She cried because—people-pleaser her—she wanted nothing other than to be a good girl. She wanted her teacher to like her. She wanted her mother to love her. She wanted to be good and to never risk that love, and here she was, being told that she had done wrong, that her mother would be upset!

It was all so silly! She was a kid! She was five and a half! Of course she was going to get messy. Of course there would be paint on her hands, and so why should there not also be paint on her pants? She was a kid and she was clumsy, and a mess like that was just a part of her life.

Her mother picked her sobbing daughter up from school,

and after much cajoling, much reassuring her that she would not abandon her, would not leave her by the side of the road to be picked up by...who exactly? She reassured her that the paint stain was fine, and that she would have a chat with Miss Willard. When your daughter's neurodivergence presents itself in anxiety, perhaps you get used to reassuring her that you love her, and when you are a mother, perhaps you never tire of doing so.

⁂

A Motes who looks like she has stepped straight out of a kindergarten classroom and into the world—a world with a lower age limit, a world where one cannot upload before one turns eighteen—is a Motes who is going to draw attention. A Motes who acts five, or seven, or twelve is a Motes who is going to inspire big feelings. She is going to inspire feelings of confusion, of alarm, of anger.

She is going to be a Motes who gets kicked from sims, who gets barred from entry. She is going to be a Motes who gets her tail stepped on, she is going to get hip-bumped out of the way, and ever they will promise it is an accident, and many times they will even be telling the truth.

She will be a Motes who gets sneered at. She will be scolded for some vague infraction, impropriety, some sin against God, against man, against the sanctity of the System. Or perhaps she will be a Motes who is studiously ignored. She will be the one others cross the street to avoid, the one others stay away from lest they be tainted with transgression by association.

She is also going to be a Motes who inspires feelings of protection, of care, of *joie de vivre.* She is going to be one who shows the hedonism in play, one whose *raison d'être* is to have fun, and inspire in others a sense of compersion for that fun. She is going to be a Motes who makes one want to play in turn. She is going to be the one you want to hold in your lap, the one you want to call adorable, the one you want to hold close and protect from pain.

✩

The inflection point came when she, the Motes who had been forked not three years prior, the Motes who was still a human who looked much like A Finger Pointing, her immediate down-tree, sat in a paint tray while painting a stage-wide sunset on a scrim.

There she was, kneeling carefully on the stage and twisting around to see the red splotch ground into the seat of her sturdy work overalls, and laughing. She laughed as she recognized the mess she had made—one big butt-print on the matte black of the stage—and she laughed at the way the paint had very clearly started to seep into the denim of her overalls. She laughed as memories flooded into her mind, of red paint on corduroy, of Miss Willard's snippy admonition, of her mother's patient re-assurances. She laughed and, rather than wave away the mess that she had made on her overalls, she lay down on her front and summoned up a smaller paintbrush instead of the roller she had been using, loaded it up with paint, and started filling in the awkward splotch on the stage into the body of some critter, round and soft. She took a break from her sunset and instead painted a fat, cartoonish skunk all in red.

By the time That It Might Give The World Orders, the play's director, found her, she had added an idealized field of grass and dandelions, had painted in a frolicking fennec fox in blue, and still lay on her front, the seat of her pants colored in red from the paint she had sat in.

Rather than admonish her like Miss Willard of the past, That It Might Give had stood in silence for a long minute, looking down at her cocladist laying down on her belly and painting with a sheepish grin on her face, and then laughed. She laughed, leaned down, and ruffled Motes's hair and then sat with her, doodling bumblebees on the stage's surface, floating up above skunk and fennec, above grass and dandelions, and sharing in memories.

✩

The process of making friends when one is a kid on a System where everyone is old and getting older is, it turns out, not the same as making friends when one is *just* old and getting older. It is an act of making two sets of friends in two different ways.

Adults feel around the edges of friendship carefully. They ask questions, they get to know each other first. They talk. They chat. They watch and observe before they decide—even if subconsciously—that they might want to be friends with their interlocutor.

Kids fall into friendship easily. They need one thing to connect on, and then they simply become friends.

They are two different ways of moving in the world, and yet they end in the same goal: friendship. A friend is a friend is a friend.

Motes fell into friendship as a kid. She fell into friendship with Alexei. She fell into friendship with Who Walks The Path. She fell into friendship with so many other kids she met at this playground or at that game sim.

Fell into and fell out of, yes? For kids fall out of friendship just as easily. They find a similarity and become the bestest of friends with each other and then that turns out to not be enough to maintain a friendship or it turns out that the other kid has another, bestester friend or it turns out that the other kid is actually kind of a b-word. And so Motes fell into friendship with Jonie who was a dog and then fell out of that friendship some few weeks later when Jonie who was a dog called Motes stinky one too many times and she was *not* stinky. She fell into friendship with Khadijah when she went through a rope skipping phase and then fell out of it when the phase ended and Khadijah cried and cried and cried and when Motes tried to rekindle the friendship the bond had already been broken. She fell out of relationships but never as many as she fell into and relationships lasted years or decades.

She fell into and out of friendships and forgot, perhaps, how to form adult friendships, and so many people she met as Big Motes only passed through her life for a week or so.

☆☆

Motes leaned hard into that memory. She leaned into the laughter and joy of painting with her fingers and, apparently, her pants, as well as the tears of fear of being abandoned for having messed up so badly.

It was not always a kid thing. She aged down her appearance, sure, falling into a comfortable vision of a twenty-something, but it was also not just an appearance thing. It was the way she acted. It was owning of playfulness as a form of hedonism, much as the rest of the fifth stanza owned hedonism as a core part of their identity.

She owned playfulness because life is play. She owned it because it was so easy to forget the role that play plays in one's life, with its carefully delineated fun times that one fits in around work and sleep and obligations. Life is play, and over time, Motes *became* play.

It changed the way that her cocladists and friends treated her. They started ruffling her hair as That It Might Give had, trying to get her excited. They started playing with her in the auditorium, hiding to jump out and startle her or running up to tap her on the shoulder and shout "You are it!" before running off to the dressing rooms to change for their role. They started doing all of the good things that one does with kids and none of the bad things. After all, if they needed Serious Motes, they could still talk to her like the fifty year old woman that she was, right?

She liked that.

✮

Slow Hours, Motes's big sister, had once had it said about her by Deny All Beginnings, town crier to her town scryer, "It seems so often to me that you have the criss-cross pattern of a school-yard tool imprinted on your face, no doubt hurled at at you by a god." She explained this to Motes that there was some contemporary interpretation of the Greek god Apollo hurling a dodgeball at the unwitting to bless them with the gift of prophecy.

And she had indeed become the prophet of the clade, the one checkered with predictions and who bore the heady scent of omens. She was the Delphic oracle to so many other prognosticators. She would get this dreamy, distant smile on her face and then she would speak. She would say, "I will tell you two truths and one lie about the future" and then she would say unnerving things that would almost certainly come to pass. Yes, they might take years to do so, but she was uncanny in her accuracy.

So Motes came to her, to the crowd of other crew, who always seemed to tolerate Slow Hours better than the cast, came to her and threw herself dramatically across her cocladist's lap, requesting some brushings to get the paint flecks out of her tail while she thought about how to say what she needed to say.

"Slow Hours, I made a friend," she said, relying on the comparatively formal name as opposed to Slow—and she was the only one from whom Slow Hours would accept that name—or Slowers to convey a bit of the gravity of the question.

"Tell me of your friend, my dear," Slow Hours replied, setting up a cone of silence.

"I met them at a dance," she said, looking down to her claws as they doodled on the stage. "I went out with Beholden and Unbidden to some crazy biker bar that was also having a mathcore band performing, and I met them in the pit."

"You were your big self, yes?"

She nodded. "We danced for a bit in the pit and then got some drinks and talked outside, then danced some more." When Slow Hours remained attentively silent, she continued. "And that was it. That is all I ever do, right? Go to a show, get wasted, maybe get laid, and then I go back to the stuff I really enjoy. I have my friends here. I have my work. I have you and Beholden and A Finger Pointing–" This was before she had openly started referring to them by familial terms. "–and Beckoning and Muse and that is all I need. I do not need much else to continue to from one day to the next. I do not *do* love or deep friendships. Not like that."

Slow Hours nodded. "I sense a 'but', Speck."

"Wellll..." Motes said, pushing herself back up to sitting. "I do not do love, but a lot of people do, including a lot of the peo-ple I wind up spending the night with in Big Motes mode. I am honest and up front, duh, and most understand that this is just for the fun of it. I am a healthy woman, right? I am, like, a cen-tury and a half old, but I am still thirty, right? I like sex as much as any hundred and fifty year old woman in her thirties."

She nodded, laughing.

"One or two have gotten big feelings for me, but most get it. We negotiate boundaries and move on with our lives. There are so many people here! It is not a big deal if someone says no that early on." Motes laughed, adding, "Once, one of them showed up here looking for me, and A Finger Pointing just about tore them in half."

Slow Hours smiled, but said gently, "You are stalling, my dear."

She groaned and buried her face against her cocladist's shoulder. "I knooow. Anyway, this person and I got started talk-ing about what we like in lasting friendships that we do not re-ally care about in one-night stands and...and they just seem like a really good person."

"And you think you might like to follow up on that?"

"They are just into all sorts of things I am. They paint—people, mostly, and some animals—and like a lot of the same music, and also...also are into the whole little thing. They sug-gested we forget the sex part and maybe do a regular sort of get-together." She hesitated before adding, far more bashfully, "You know. As kids."

"Have you told A Finger Pointing about them?"

She shook her head. "That was part of what I wanted to talk to you about."

Slow Hours asked her several questions. She asked about the person. She asked about the day before. She asked about the morning after. She asked about Beholden and Unbidden and the crowd around her. She asked about how drunk she had been, how high. She asked like there was some thread being tugged, whether by her fingers or by Motes's or by Apollo himself. No one ever asked how this worked, not even Slow Hours—*especially* not Slow Hours—lest the whole thing come tumbling down.

"Speck," she said, interrupting Motes at one point. "Here are two truths and a lie."

Motes frowned.

"One: they are a fucking creep."

There was a moment's silence before she giggled nervously, a fawning laugh. The flow of prophecy had a rhythm, though, and so she remained silent to let Slow Hours continue.

"Two: you are lonely. You have us, yes. You have your stanza and the rest of the troupe. You have your family and your work, but what you do not have are the types of friends you describe. You are friendly with everyone here, everyone is your friend, but you do not *have* many friends in this way."

Still wrong-footed, Motes leaned away from her cocladist. "And the third?"

"Three: much of this is our fault."

" 'Yours' as in the clade's?"

After a moment, Slow Hours spoke again, the knife-edge of prophecy letting off of her throat. "There are as many reasons to keep someone for yourself as there are ways to do so. The whole of the fifth stanza—and, to a lesser extent, the whole of Au Lieu de Rêve—has closed around you. Not tight, of course, we are not keeping you trapped and hidden away, but we are all intensely, intensely protective of you. We have all endeavored to make your life here the best that it can be, as you have invited us to do. This was part of our conversations going all the way back, was it not? That you enjoyed leaning into being cared for, and we enjoyed having someone to collectively care for? We do not like creeps around our Motes, and so we see creeps everywhere."

Once Motes saw what she was saying, saw through the everblue tint of prophecy and her own little game of two truths and a lie, the skunk's shoulders relaxed and she slumped against her cocladist, sniffling.

"We all love you, Speck. That is all."

Motes understood after some days of consideration that it was not her prophecy. It was theirs. It was Slow Hours's and A Finger Pointing's and Beholden's and Unbidden's and the whole rest of Au Lieu Du Rêve's.

She was still good friends with Alexei, that kid who was not a creep, never had been a creep, years later. Him and so many more.

✰⋆

Motes should not, she is told, do many things.

She should not look too much like a child. She should not look like a kid because there are those with paraphilias surrounding children, and this would be both potentially harmful to her, as well as to the optics of the Ode clade as a whole.

She should not act too much like a child. She should not act like a kid because, while a focus on play is all well and good, a sense of maturity would keep her grounded in the world around her while leaning into childhood would not, and would potentially be harmful to the optics of the Ode clade as a whole.

She should not treat her stanza as family. She should not treat her down-tree as her mother, nor A Finger Pointing's partner, Beholden, as a parent, nor Slow Hours and Time Rushes as her sisters, the rest of the fifth stanza as siblings throughout, because family dynamics within one extended definition of a singular person create more room for potentially unhealthy modes of interaction, just as might intraclade romantic relationships, and this might also potentially be harmful to the optics of the Ode clade as a whole.

Motes should not, she is told, do many things, and yet she does them anyway. She is careful. She is gradual. She has allies.

She is told these things via hints and intimations. She is told these things through A Finger Pointing and Slow Hours and countless others.

She is told gently. She is told to be careful. She is told out of a sense of protectiveness. She is told because, regardless of the implications of these warnings, the fifth stanza really does love her—they tell her and she believes them—and she is told because even she can see many ways that there are plenty and sufficient reasons that someone looking young in a world with a lower bound on age would be viewed with disdain, and yet she may not see *all* of those ways.

✶

Above all else, Motes enjoyed piggyback rides.

☆

Whenever Motes would visit Michelle/Sasha, or she would visit Le Rêve, their neighborhood sim, Motes would slow down. She would not tame her joy, nor tamp down her ebullience, but she would gentle the way she moved, the way she acted, the way she touched. The hugs that she gave Sasha/Michelle were soft and comfortable and unhurried. They were the hugs one gave an elder, perhaps, but they were no less full of love for it. They were not hugs of obligation, but of care.

After all, some secret part of her reasoned, even little skunks need a grandma, though this was a term she never spoke aloud.

Their relationship was as friends, as companions or comrades. They shared a childhood together. They had the same parents and teachers. They remembered so many of the same things from youth. They remembered so many of the same people. They remembered Miss Willard together, red paint ground into corduroy.

Their relationship was as friends, and as Motes grew into who she became, the ways in which this presented shifted to accommodate such.

It was Michelle/Sasha who pulled forth the memories of flower crowns from within Motes and set them so brightly before her. It was her that was the reason they so often adorned Motes's head, both Big and Little. Dandelion crown upon dandelion crown graced her hair or mane after Sasha/Michelle first made her one some two centuries back.

It was after that that Motes made a promise to herself that she would visit her root instance—or invite her to visit in turn—at least once a year.

Michelle/Sasha very rarely wore claw or nail polish, thanks to the shifting of her form, but when she did, it was Motes who applied it to nails or claws, the two of them laying beside each other on a picnic blanket in the warm sunlight, sharing in quiet and comfort and conversation of only the small things. What had Motes been painting? When had Debarre last visited Sasha/Michelle in the field? Who among the clade do you suppose was most likely to dye their hair or fur some wild color?

They would talk of the small things and, when all claws or nails had been colored pink or blue or ever-shifting waves of green, they would roll onto their backs and pick out shapes in the clouds and Michelle/Sasha would tell Motes all of the things she would have done with her kids, had she had any. Flower crowns: a must. Story time: most definitely. Sleepovers and pillow-forts: a thousand times yes.

All of these and more Motes provided for her in spades as chances, occasions, opportunities.

Motes would explain all of the ways she would get in trouble—lying? Check. Punching a boy for calling her stinky? Check. Drawing on the walls? Check, in bold-face and italics—and for each one of them, Sasha/Michelle would counter with the most poetic of punishments: when Motes lied, she would make her live within a cone of silence for a whole day, so that no untruths could be heard. When Motes punched a boy for calling her stinky, Michelle/Sasha would take her with when she went shopping for perfumes and make her smell each and every one of them. When Motes drew on the walls, why, all other projects would need to be put on hold and she would simply have to keep going until every inch of the room was covered with the most beautiful art she had ever seen.

And while none of these ever came to pass, Motes loved her all the more for it.

After Sasha/Michelle had quit, Motes slept with Beholden and A Finger Pointing every night for nearly three months and talked only ever of such love that was now gone from the world.

✩

But always, Motes played.

She played because play was transgressive for one such as her, was it not? Oh, there were games sys-side. Within her own clade was a game designer and curator, What Gifts—and she often leaned on Motes for input and play-testing—and so of course play was okay, but as soon as one presents oneself as she did, as a child, then suddenly that play becomes something that works to define that very part of her and thus vice versa, her childishness casts that play in a childish light. It was transgressive because when Motes played, it cast the play that every adult around her engaged with as either defined by or contrasted against her very presence.

But she played in that transgression. She used it to push and press against those definitions and boundaries. She played as a twenty-something, letting her cocladists and coworkers ruffle her hair to rile her up or jump from behind a curtain to scare her.

She played as a child—even if, at first, it was only within the confines of home, and then within the stanza's neighborhood, and then within the troupe, before she ever did so in public.

She played in that familial identity, of A Finger Pointing as 'Ma' and Beholden as 'Bee' and Slow Hours as Sis Hours—even if, at first, it was only within the confines of home; even if, at first, it engendered awkward and cautious feelings.

Life is but a walking shadow, a player poor that struts and frets upon the stage, yes? All the world is a stage, and all the men and women merely players, yes?

Motes played because life was a play.

But even as she tested those boundaries and always respected them when they were set, she would ever negotiate a way forward such that she could live this life that she had set for herself.

It was a bit, and she was committed to it. She was an actress, yes? She had a part to play, yes? The kid? The child? The daughter and sister, yes? It was method acting over the course of a lifetime. She committed to the bit and convinced herself as best she could to forget how to uncommit, and that, in itself was lovely.

✩

Motes dreamed.

She dreamed and dreamed and dreamed, her mind wandering over her past, there in the dark, there alone, after A Finger Pointing left, there in her extra soft bed with her overstuffed duvet and all of her stuffed animals.

At some point, hours or days or perhaps mere minutes later, she slept and dreamed true. She dreamed that she was sitting in a field of well-tended grass that was nonetheless dotted liberally with dandelions, speckled with bumblebees. She dreamed that she had all the wonder of a child and that the day was sunny and lovely and the grass was inviting her to roll around in it, and just above, just in the distance, a hyperblack rectangle, a hole in the world that hungrily devoured all of the light that it could, lingered, and it was neither good nor bad, and even with its insatiable hunger, the day was sunny and lovely and the grass was inviting her to roll around in it.

And then she awoke.

# A Finger Pointing — 2362

# 7

A Finger Pointing was not playing.

She was not fucking around. She was not putting up with this. She would never put up with this, never *should* have put up with this. Seven years of silence, five decades of barely concealed spying, a century of awkward attempts to maintain a friendship, a cohesion, a sense of community with someone who clearly loathed some integral part of her life.

She was not going to play around, here. She was not going to play soft. She was not even going to play hard: she was not going to play at all. Not with Hammered Silver. Not anymore.

> **To:** Time Is A Finger Pointing At Itself of the Ode clade **(EYES-ONLY)**
> **From:** Memory Is A Mirror Of Hammered Silver of the Ode clade
> **On:** systime 238+291
>
> Time Is A Finger Pointing At Itself,
>
> I am breaking my communication embargo to write you regarding some concerns that I have on the current state of the clade, the fifth stanza, and And We Are The Motes In The Stage-Lights.

Upon learning that I Remember The Rattle Of The Dry Grass has continued in her association with you, And We Are The Motes In The Stage-Lights, and the one who has named herself Sasha, I have instituted a no-contact order between her and the rest of the sixth stanza for her perfidy. It was my hope that my previous directive regarding the fifth stanza would have been clear enough to require no further clarification, and yet this is the situation that we have found ourselves in.

This letter serves as a means to reinforce that this no-contact order still stands. That I even need to send such a reminder is upsetting and insulting. I have sent a letter to And We Are The Motes In The Stage-Lights explaining my reasoning more clearly for someone who seems obstinately opposed to staying grounded in reality. I will reiterate the status of this request here for clarity:

1. There is to be no contact between the fifth stanza and either the sixth or seventh stanzas.
2. There is to be no contact between the one who has named herself Sasha and either the sixth or seventh stanzas.
3. There is to be no contact between I Remember The Rattle Of Dry Grass and the rest of the sixth stanza until further notice.

I expect better from Odists. Perhaps my expectations are misguided.

—Memory Is A Mirror Of Hammered Silver of the Ode clade.

⭑⭒

One treacherously sunny afternoon some centuries back, Sasha/Michelle Hadje sat tiredly on the edge of a fountain in the middle of a brick-paved pedestrian mall. Just a woman or a skunk or perhaps both sitting on the rough stone in classical white, head bowed in exhaustion and concentration as the sun warmed the back of her neck. Beside her sat a man, a politician, watching as she drained her reserves of reputation to bring into being ten more instances of herself, each blissfully unafflicted by the restlessness-of-shape and in many ways less affected by the restlessness-of-mind that plagued her, though never completely without.

"So, what next?" the man asked.

"What is next is that I get assignments from the Council and then take a fucking vacation," she replied. "I plan on sleeping for at least three days straight."

He laughed. "I wholeheartedly endorse this course of action. One of you want to take on an assignment today?"

They—this gaggle of skunks and women who were still in some way skunks—put their heads together to discuss, and even then, even so few minutes after they had come into being and taken for their names the first lines of the ten stanzas of a poem each held close to their heart, it became clear that they differed in some fundamental way that went beyond simple individuation.

Time Is A Finger Pointing At Itself, the woman who bore the first line of the fifth stanza for a name, had lived through this four times, enough times to know just what had been done, for had she not been Michelle/Sasha for the first four first lines coming into being?

Sasha/Michelle had sat on the rim of the fountain and looked out on the world with tired eyes and wondered at the simple beauty of Old Town Square, the brick pavers and the gas lamps and the twee shops, and forked her first long-lived instance, I Am At A Loss For Images In This End Of Days of the Ode clade.

Michelle/Sasha had remembered a day two decades back when she had sat on the rim of a fountain not so different from this one, sat beside an erstwhile partner who made such a better friend than lover that they remained in love in friendship in their own gentle way until ey had given emself to the act of creation, and forked into her second long-lived instance, Life Breeds Life But Death Must Now Be Chosen.

Sasha/Michelle had thought of their conversation together, those two better-friends-than-lovers, about some musical her grandparents had taken her to for her birthday, how she had sung out of key, *"Oh, my Rivkah, where have you gone?"* then hid her face behind her coffee cup, and forked off her third long-lived instance, Oh, But To Whom Do I Speak These Words.

Michelle/Sasha had smiled at the memories of how she had, despite her poor attempt at expressing the joy of that song, gushed about nearly every aspect of the production, the use of projectors to add a visual dreaminess to the stage, the subtle use of props as percussion instruments, and forked again into her fourth long-lived instance, Among Those Who Create Are Those Who Forge.

And at last, Sasha/Michelle remembered how, even after she fell silent, she and her friend had sat in the glow of the sun, thinking about just how wonderful a time she had had—her directly, her friend in compersion—seeing so complete an experience of a well-produced musical, and forked into her, into Time Is A Finger Pointing At Itself.

She was forked smiling.

And so when this man, this politician, this Jonas asked who wanted an assignment, she had decided instead to linger in that joy, to remember that lovely day instead of searching for some way to reengage with politics. That was left to The Only Time I Know My True Name Is When I Dream, the first line of the eighth stanza. She did not know what compelled True Name to lean into politics as she had been forked after A Finger Pointing, but she wished her all the best.

When Michelle/Sasha stood at last, swaying, and tottered towards the remainder of her newly-formed clade, these ten emanations bearing in their heart some secret, individual joy bestowed upon them by their tired creator, they had all welcomed her into their presence as a first-among-equals and bore her away to home, to her field of grass and dandelions.

What followed was a conversation that lasted until dusk. Each of them minus True Name, already at work, talked about the experience of coming into being, the experience of being settled firmly into one shape unlike their root instance, about the things that they loved and what they might do with that love.

They had not existed for a day and yet A Finger Pointing still loved them each and loved them all together.

She learned of all of their different focuses and kept them straight in her head that she might know them better later, but also she watched how each of them moved, how each of them acted. She kept in mind all that they talked about so that she might share it with True Name.

Hammered Silver was there. She was the one who, after Sasha/Michelle had tired of walking and requested to sit down, had offered her lap as a pillow that she might dote on her down-tree. There was such love in her eyes, such maternal love, for this woman who was at once herself and not. She did not smile, but cooed in concern as a mother might to some crying child. A Finger Pointing made note of this, too, for, yes, she also felt that concern, but also to see such in someone so like herself was a joy in its own right.

From that point on, A Finger Pointing made herself the glue of this growing clade. She would share weekly or monthly lunches and dinners with each, keeping up with them via letters and, once they were implemented, sensorium messages. Even as her smile remained or veered towards a smirk or wily grin, even as her opinions on each of her cocladists grew more com-plicated, watching burgeoning loves and animosities, she kept in touch.

✩

Yes, there were steps that she needed to take. There were ways that she needed to keep herself safe. There were ways that those who above all else she loved might come to harm and she needed to keep them safe as well. She needed to ensure their safety even above her own.

Dry Grass was the first she kept safe. A home was provided to her within the fifth stanza's neighborhood, a little cottage some doors down from where A Finger Pointing, Beholden, and Motes lived. She may have been safe where she was, they both agreed, but safety from her down-tree's anger was not the only safety that was needed. There was also safety from being alone, from being left without support.

Dry Grass did not weep. She did not sob. The tears she shed that night, sitting around the kitchen table with A Finger Pointing and Beholden, were tears of fury. They were tears of betrayal.

The next day, they worked together.

They reconvened around that same kitchen table, though this time, instead of Beholden, Sasha joined them, the cinnamon skunk holding a mug of coffee—one of those mochas she so loved—in her paws, staring down into the remnants of the whipped cream that remained atop.

"I am sorry to hear that, Dry Grass. I am sorry to both of you," she said.

Both nodded.

"Is there anything to do about it?" Dry Grass asked. "I do not need to go back. I do not need her back in my life. What I do need, though, is to know if we need to respond in any particular way."

"It has been more than a few years since I have spoken to Hammered Silver," Sasha admitted. "I last spoke with her around the time that the Artemisians arrived, yes? Before I became that which I am, yes?" A faint smirk painted her muzzle as she added, "The one who has named herself Sasha, yes?"

A Finger Pointing gritted her teeth, counting silently to ten. "That she weaponized all of our names against us only makes me all the angrier. I do not know what to expect of her, though. I do not know what her true intent is."

"As in what is her goal for sending this letter?"

"Yes. Ostensibly, it is to simply tell me that Dry Grass has been ostracized, but I do not imagine that that is the *only* reason."

Dry Grass snorted. "She is an Odist; of course it is not. I am only sorry that I tuned her out for so many years, or I might have a better idea of precisely what, though."

"She is an Odist, yes," Sasha said. "She is not a bad person, but neither is she by necessity good, and now we are seeing the wickedness of which we are all capable in particular. Similarly, though, I do not have an answer for you. She has been inaccessible to me for sixteen years now, and before that, I was too distracted to spend much time engaging with her."

A Finger Pointing sighed, slouching back against the chair. "That is okay, my dear. You have had no easier a time of it than the rest of us. Decidedly worse, actually."

Sasha laughed.

"Still, can you at least tell us if you believe there is anything that we need to worry about?"

"Worry?" The skunk took a moment to think as she lapped at a bit more of the whipped cream. "Are you asking after danger? Are you asking if she might make your name anathema or find someone to hunt you down with a vial of CPV?"

Her two cocladists tensed. Neither wished to contend with the thought that Hammered Silver might have it in her to kill anyone in the only way the System knew how, some object loaded up with a contraproprioceptive virus to pierce their very being and crash them entire. However, though neither wished to, they both had to, and so they both nodded.

Sasha smiled reassuringly. "I do not believe you need worry about *that*. Making your name anathema would taint her own reputation, would it not? And she does seem rather more concerned about that than anything. She is mad, yes, and perhaps feeling betrayed, but she is not feeling murderous. She does not have that within her, I do not think. Would you like me to check all the same?"

Dry Grass nodded.

"Will it put you at risk?" A Finger Pointing asked earnestly. "It is not worth that."

"Not at all, no. I have limited contact with the eighth stanza still. They are careful, of course, but I can ask When I Dream a yes or no question and expect one ping for no, two for yes."

"Please do, then."

The skunk bowed and then let her gaze drift briefly around the kitchen, unseeing, while she sent her question via sensorium message. It took all of thirty seconds before she returned her focus to A Finger Pointing and Dry Grass, grinning. "More than just a no, When I Dream let me hear eir laughter at the very idea. You are *quite* safe from that."

The others both sighed, then laughed at the shared relief.

"Thank you, my dear," Dry Grass said, reaching out to rest a hand on the skunk's forearm. "That is incredibly helpful. We may still wish to ask Waking World—if he will still speak with us, that is—but that does mean a lot."

Sasha smiled and patted the back of that hand. "Of course. If I am able to soothe your worries any further, I will do so. This is, I must say, fucking bullshit."

⁂

To fall in love with a cocladist is to engage in a radical form of self-love. To fall in love with a cocladist is to find the ways in which perhaps you *are* your type. To fall in love with a cocladist is to accept that you are large; you contain multitudes. To fall in love with your cocladist is to recognize that your hyperfixations define, in part, your sense of self, and that if you expand beyond one hyperfixation, then perhaps you can be more than just one self.

A Finger Pointing forked all nine of her up-tree instances in systime 3, back in the early days when it still cost to fork. She had plans, though, and she had a way around those costs. She forked once, leaving her and her new instance with half of her original reputation, less than it would cost to fork again, and then her new instance simply granted the reputation back to her, enough to fork once more. She had a way around those costs, for in those days, back before the reputation market had patched out that particular glitch, her up-tree instances did not need reputation beyond hers. She had plans. She had ideas for her particular joy. She would lean into theatre, build a troupe made up of just herself, for surely there were ten roles that needed to be filled in running a theatre.

There was her, the executive director and administrator.

There was That It Might Give The World Orders, the director.

There was The World Is An Audience Before A Stage, the educator within and without.

There was Where It Watches The Slow Hours Progress, the script manager and librarian.

There was And We Are The Motes In The Stage-Lights, the set and prop designer.

There was Beholden To The Heat Of The Lamps, the sound and music director.

There was If I Walk Backward, Time Moves Forward, who explored interactivity in art.

There was If I Walk Forward, Time Rushes On, the dancer and choreographer.

There was If I Stand Still, The World Moves Around Me, the stage manager who dabbled in lights.

There was And The Only Constant Is Change, an actor with a penchant for death scenes and just plain strange bird.

And they all acted, and they all promoted, and they all taught and helped as techs and loved each other. They were all hedonists, to the last, because A Finger Pointing was a hedonist, one who wanted to enjoy life to the fullest and to be everybody's friend.

She spent time with them all, yes, but the benefit of diving deep into music is that Beholden began to seek out live shows and concerts, and so when A Finger Pointing spent time with her, they became events. They started to veer perilously close to dates.

At some point, though they disagreed on when—was it five years later? Ten? Each argued passionately for one, and then the other—they *became* dates.

There was sense of aromancy in A Finger Pointing that grew after she forked. She never could say where from; perhaps it was simply that she would rather have been friends with every-one than foster a particular friendship with one person. And yet there was something about Beholden. Something fulfilling, per-haps, or complementary, or a self-love that rose above all others.

And so they fell in love, each in their own way. They fell in love and, for the most part, reveled. Yes, they had their spats, their breaks from each other. Yes, they had their flings besides, and the occasional relationship, all negotiated and cherished and bound up in compersion. But always they had each other.

There were, of course, the social implications to consider, the taboo around intraclade relationships, the implications of narcissism and other, far more crass terms. Suggestions were made from on high, such as it were, from across the clade.

True Name suggested. She suggested that, as pleased as she was for them—and she *was* pleased!—their relationship remain something for behind closed doors. Something where they kept their I-love-yous and kisses for a shared bed rather than out on the town or at however many gatherings they might wish to go to. Politics was, as ever, politics, and here are the political rea-sons laid bare. Jonas had, after all, set the plan before her after he had already spun it into being, and even she was beholden to it, much as it rankled for her, too. Much as it would decades later nearly the death of her.

Hers were the kind suggestions. The comprehensible sug-gestions. The ones based in logic and explained clearly: main-taining a sense of taboo in what was quickly becoming a queer-normative society added to the desire for change by providing something to reach for. Comprehensible, yes; the logic was sound, internally consistent. Wrong, of course, but if such was to be the way of things in this plan-twisted world, if such were the optics to which they were all held to account, then so be it. Such were the optics to which they were all held to account.

True Name, ever her friend, made her kind suggestions, hugged her, and reassured her of her camaraderie.

Other suggestions: not so kind.

For there was Hammered Silver, strangely quiet during one of A Finger Pointing's many lunch dates with her. Quiet and distant, all conversation polite and full of nothing comments about the sim, the soup, the coffee, all gazes cast upon everything but her.

When pressed, she had simply shrugged and offered some plainly false words about being distracted and begged an end to the meal.

A Finger Pointing hardly needed to wait for some explanation more true, for when she arrived home—home to that apartment building, home to the simple and cozy unit that Beholden had only moved into a few weeks prior—there was an envelope waiting for her, taped unceremoniously to her door. In it were words of scorn, a sense of a nose pointed snootily up into the air as though to escape some rancid smell.

Did she not know what she was doing? Did she—A Finger Pointing! One of the first lines!—not consider the optics of an intraclade relationship for the rest of her stanza? The rest of the clade? Really, *the* A Finger Pointing ought to know better.

It was the first letter of several. It was the first time of many that she stood stock still, seethed, and counted to ten before opening her door to greet Beholden—her partner regardless of Hammered Silver's haughty implications—with her usual jaunty smile once more firmly in place.

⁂

A Weapon Against The Waking World, it turned out, was perfectly happy to meet with them.

Waking World had long ago taken up the mantle of 'dad'. Not father, not guardian, but specifically *dad*. Where Hammered Silver reveled in feelings of motherhood, of caring and cherishing and clinging tight, such as they might be sys-side, he had reveled in all the glorious humor of fatherhood, of protecting and uplifting and letting go. He was a being of idle quips and truly terrible dad jokes. He was a man who might call you 'sport' or 'champ' as easily as 'friend'. He was, in all ways except physical, *your* dad, whoever you might be.

He had long ago taken the form of a stocky man, hairline receding, tall enough, looking just enough like an Odist that one could see that he might belong to the clade—his name aside, of course—and yet the resemblance was slight enough that seeing him beside Hammered Silver would not inspire comments of "siblings...?"

He was not beside her now.

The first thing that he did upon arriving at the Au Lieu Du Rêve library—a location carefully chosen for the ease with which it might be secured—was to open his arms to Dry Grass and, when she dashed to him, wrap her up in a hug.

Once he had guided her to one of the overstuffed chairs and she had had her cry—one of relief, this time, rather than fury or despair—he pulled up a seat to join the loose circle within the solarium.

"Wifey is pissed," he began, then laughed. "I called her that and she hit me so hard I saw stars. Usually, I just get a *look*."

A Finger Pointing sat bolt upright. "*What?!*"

"Jesus," Dry Grass whispered, eyes wide.

He shrugged. "It is not the first time."

Beholden, leaning back with her arms crossed over her chest, snorted. "Great," she said. "I know that Sasha said that she was not an existential threat, but apparently we still have to worry about violence."

He held up his hands and shook his head. "No, no, I do not think you do. She hit me because that is the relationship that we have."

" 'Relationship'?"

"Yes. A lover's spat. Despite how often we say 'I love you' or the fact that we share a bed, despite the fact that I *do* earnestly love her, she remains staunchly of the opinion that we are in no way in a relationship."

"Okay, but how can you love her after all she has done?" the skunk snapped. A Finger pointing rested a hand on her paw, but she continued regardless. "Motes is fucking catatonic in bed now. She cut us all off, cut off whole stanzas, cut off the Bălans. Now she has cut off Dry Grass—one of her own—and here you are, skulking into the library because you know that she cannot track you here."

Waking World averted his gaze. "That is not how love works,

Beholden. I do not like what she has done. I *hate* what she has done. I wish that I could get to know Motes better, even, but I do love her, and my position in our little game is...precarious. I must be careful."

"Bullshit."

"My muse," A Finger Pointing murmured. "I know that you are angry. We are all angry. Hell, I am *livid,* but this needs to be a conversation for another time. Right now, there are too many pieces in play."

Beholden subsided, lips still curled in a snarl. After a moment's silence, her shoulders slumped and she looked away, resting her paw atop A Finger Pointing's hand. "Yes, of course. I am sorry, Waking World. I was the one who found Motes overflowing. She was covered in blood from getting hit in the nose or something, and was all scraped up. It was...hard on me, is all."

Waking World blanched. "Wait, shit, really? Uh..." He folded his hands in his lap and frowned down to them. "Shit. I am sorry, Beholden. I did not know."

She nodded. "None of us know why, but we are asking around to see if anyone knows what happened. It could be she just fell or something. I imagine the letter she got must have been a hell of a shock." She smiled faintly, shakily. "I apologize, though, earnestly. That should not have spilled over onto you."

He nodded, giving a hint of a bow from where he sat. "Well," he started once more. "All of that to say that she is mad as hell, but in a very *her* way. She is feeling mad at Dry Grass for visiting and mad at herself for the decision she made—I do not think even she agrees with it—so she is just getting mad at every little thing. That is probably why she sent off that flurry of letters."

"Flurry?" A Finger Pointing asked, frowning.

"I got one too," Dry Grass said. "Probably five or six pages of yelling at me, yelling about all of you, and just plain yelling."

Waking World shrugged. "She even sent me one. I got it while in the next room over from her."

"Jesus Christ," A Finger Pointing said, laughing. "She really *is* mad."

"Right. Sasha is right, though, you do not need to worry about any existential threat from her. She is not going to come hunting any of you down. She is not going to do anything but seethe."

"Is that something we need to be concerned about, though?" she asked. "Beholden is not the only one worried about her getting violent."

"Really, no, I do not think you have anything like that to worry about from her." Rubbing his palms together, he leaned forward to rest his elbows on his knees. "I might, but that is my role in this: I rein her in by being a target."

"Well, is there anything we can do about it, then? I do not like your role in this either, but again, that will be a conversation for later. I find myself all but blind with fury, though, and the thought that I might just let this slide back into silence is unconscionable. Were she to allow us to be in the same room..." She trailed off, letting the aposiopesis speak for her.

"I am half tempted to find a way back just to give her a punch to the gut, if she is hitting you," Dry Grass growled. "But I have been locked out of the entire sim."

Waking World laughed weakly. "Please do not do that, my dear. That is not what anyone needs right now, least of all her."

"What *does* she need, then?"

"She needs to feel like she has hurt you," he said, speaking slowly. "She needs to know that her words had the power to do that, since silence did not work. She needs to feel like she accomplished something through them."

"She *did* hurt us, though," A Finger Pointing said flatly. She could feel a wave of dissociation, of vertigo. She pushed it down so that she could continue. "She hurt Motes—quite literally. She hurt Dry Grass, and she re-traumatized us all all over again. I would say that she succeeded admirably."

He shrugged helplessly.

"Well, I ask again, then: can we do anything about it?"

They sat in silence for nearly a minute while Waking World thought. A Finger Pointing gave Beholden's paw a squeeze before retrieving her hand once more. Her sensorium felt like it was lit up with fairy lights and arc lamps, a gently twirling Christmas tree of a self. She could hear the rushing of water, and much of what she was seeing was beginning to blur, but she forced herself to remain as present as she was able, turning her senses down as much as she could get away with in the moment.

"Hammered Silver is having a tantrum," he said at last. "She does not want to argue with you. She will not be convinced because she does not really care if anything changes. She does not *want* anything to change, I think. She does not want to win. She just wants to be angry and she just wants you to hurt."

"A *tantrum?!*" Beholden cried, then quickly and visibly tamped down her temper. "She is having a tantrum? A tantrum does not lead to bleeding children."

Waking World once more raised his hands in placation. "I

cannot speak to that, Beholden, I promise. What I *can* promise is that she would never strike anyone." He winced, his previous words standing in immediate contrast. "Well, okay. I, uh…all that to say, I do not know what happened to Motes, but I cannot believe that it was her doing."

Furrowing her brow, A Finger Pointing nodded to Beholden, feeling her sense of the world lag behind. "I am with Waking World on that. I cannot believe she would do that, herself, and we do not know what happened to Motes, may not until she returns to us," she said slowly, then let her gaze shift over to him. "But I am also with Beholden on her incredulity. What does it mean to have such a tantrum? What cruelty goes into wanting us to hurt?"

"I do not know, A Finger Pointing," he said, lowering his hands to rub them over his knees. "I try to hold her back. I try to mellow her role."

"What even *is* her role?" Beholden asked.

"Family," he said, then rushed to continue, heading off complaints about the family before him. "She focuses on the idea of familial connections between sys- and phys-side, how people maintain them, how families deal with relatives uploading."

"Do found families not count?" Beholden sneered.

"They do, but she is…prescriptive about them."

The skunk snorted.

"No–" A Finger Pointing paused, regained her sense of self for a moment, continued. "No, Beholden, it is as internally consistent as Jonas's thoughts on intraclade relationships. It makes sense, it is just wrong. It hurts for us—and it *does* hurt, Waking World, she has succeeded in that—because we have our own internally consistent view that she doubtless sees as just as wrong. We just do not throw tantrums that lead to such pain. We hate less."

"For as much as she apparently hates Motes, she sure is being a fucking child about this," Beholden mumbled.

A Finger Pointing laughed bitterly. "You are not wrong, my love. Motes at her youngest has never thrown a tantrum quite like this. Do we just drop it, then? Let her feel superior?"

"That would certainly work," he said, shrugging. "I do not know how much it would accomplish for your feelings, but she would leave you alone. She really does just want to feel like she is in the right, and no amount of argument will make her feel anything but justified."

"Yeah, fuck that," Beholden said, to which Dry Grass nodded emphatically.

"Fuck that, indeed," A Finger Pointing said. She could feel just how inadvisable the attitude was as the words left her mouth, could feel her control slipping, and yet she had her role to play, her guardianship to uphold.

"Well, whatever you do," Waking World said cautiously, "be careful. Keep yourselves safe above all else. If not from her, then at least from your own anger."

She nodded and pushed herself slowly to her feet through a wave of unreality, of derealization, swaying for a moment. "We will," she said, bowing to him and turning to Beholden. "My dear, I am quite done, will you take me home?"

✩

Letter after letter, topic after topic. They became rote. They

became routine. They became a signature of Hammered Silver after every little decision that A Finger Pointing made which did not meet her standards. Every little decision that *anyone* made, if what True Name and Praiseworthy had to say was true.

And it was not just her, after all, was it?

For better or worse, she was the representative of her stanza. She was a synecdoche: she *was* the fifth stanza. Anything that the stanza did, whether as a whole or individually, she would hear about through those tetchy letters, those little missives Hammered Silver saw fit to send her.

A note here: *Surely The Only Constant can find some less dramatic way to depict death on stage; has ey no thought for how that might reflect on the rest of us as so public a clade?*

*A message there: Beholden To The Flow Of The Crowds was seen punching someone at The Party. I would ask that you inform her of our standards of behavior.*

It became something of a joke—granted, mostly to herself, for she rarely shared any of these messages with others. Even True Name thought less of optics than Hammered Silver. Even the politician! These notes began to feel like letters to the editor for some small-town newspaper: semi-public complaints about propriety that left a sour whiff of entitlement in the air behind them.

And yet their apparent friendship continued. Somehow, against all odds, they continued to meet weekly for years, for decades. They would find some dainty cafe in an equally dainty neighborhood in the middle of some enormous city serving wine and sandwiches on baguettes. They would find some twee farm stand in the middle of millions of acres of carefully curated land serving the best fucking salad either of them had ever tasted. They would stand in the middle of nowhere, some flat plane of an unfinished sim with a single, incredibly detailed tree right in the 'middle' of all that nothing, with lunches they packed for the occasion.

They would meet up and they would talk, and A Finger Pointing would swallow enough of her frustration with the letters to maintain this friendship without compromising her morals.

But at some point, even the closest of friendships find a point of irreconcilable difference. There is a point at which there is no way to agree upon a topic, and one must choose: do we agree to disagree? Do we argue forever and hate it? Do we argue forever and turn it into a cherished pastime? Do we simply part ways? Even the closest of friendships must confront this decision.

Theirs was not the closest of friendships.

One day, sometime some few years into the 2200s, sometime around systime 100, there was a point where the tenor of these meetings once more changed. Once more, there was a distance, a stiffness, and when pressed, once more nothing came from it.

No letter came.

The next meeting was much the same.

No letter came.

The next meeting was canceled: "I am not feeling well."

Fair enough, there were days when A Finger Pointing did not feel well, were there not? Sickness, a thing of the past, nonetheless still appeared psychosomatically, or perhaps Hammered Silver was going through one of the spells each of the Odists had been left with, those little bits of overflowing when being oneself became too much and overrode whatever it meant to exist and the world was too noisy to see and too bright to hear. Perhaps Hammered Silver was overflowing.

The next meeting was canceled: "I am still unwell." Well, okay. At times The Only Constant would be taken out for weeks at a time, desperately clinging to life despite death a thing of the past. A Finger Pointing sent a get-well-soon note and a dichroic rose to her home sim.

The next meeting was canceled, and this time, the note was: "I have a prior engagement."

This was bullshit, patented and trademarked, registered as a copyright and service mark. A prior engagement, indeed! Did she think that A Finger Pointing was a brand new upload? Did she think that her cocladist was really so stupid? The Odists! The Odists not forking! Were Hammered Silver a member of the tenth stanza—were Hammered Silver actually Death Itself, that most lovely of people—perhaps she could understand, but she was not. She was not! Hammered Silver had laughed countless times before over the sudden disappearance of the need to worry about 'prior engagements'.

A Finger Pointing knew this was bullshit, and she also knew that Hammered Silver knew this, knew that she knew it was bullshit.

*"Hammered Silver, my dear, I would rest much easier if I knew what was happening,"* she sent over a sensorium message.

The reply: *"Oh, you know how it goes. One simply overbooks oneself. Let us meet next week at the usual time, yes?"*

And so she agreed, and so at last they met, and once more there was a stiffness and closed off nature about Hammered Silver.

"Okay, Hammered Silver," she said, sitting back with her tiny (and frankly far too bitter) espresso in hand. "I really would like to know what it is that is happening. Often, there have been chilly moments between us, but rarely one so enduring or one that includes avoiding each other."

"Really, my dear, it is nothing," Hammered Silver said. "I was feeling unwell, and then I had a prior engagement."

"And the meetings before?"

Hammered Silver only looked out the window, expression blank, unreadable.

"Hammered Silver," A Finger Pointing said gently, putting

every ounce of gentle earnestness, soft coaxing, heartfelt concern into her voice that she could manage. "If you were feeling unwell, I wish that I had been able to in some way help."

No answers were forthcoming.

She ran through recent events in her mind and, finding nothing, began to run through events from months past, the last year.

Ah.

"This is about Motes, then?"

The wrinkle that appeared dead center between Hammered Silver's eyebrows made a rather efficient reply.

A Finger Pointing sighed. "Please, my dear. I would love to be able to address your concerns about Motes, but I cannot do so unless you tell me what they are."

And so she did. She laid out several points about what she felt described Motes's behavior as inappropriate. The lack of children on the System. The existence of pedophilia. The baseless accusations that Lagrange had been a haven for pedophiles. The reception that others who presented themselves as children had received. Point after point after point.

They all boiled down to yet more of the same. Optics and optics and optics. Even True Name thought less about optics than Hammered Silver. Even the politician.

The lunch date ran long and A Finger Pointing grew weary of discussing point after point after point, talking about optics and optics and optics. There were no refutations that made a dent in the argument.

In the end, Hammered Silver let out a frustrated sigh and said, "We may continue to meet, my friend, but only on the condition that we do not speak further of Motes."

She blinked, taken aback. They had ever spoken of any and all things without holding aught back. At least, so far as she knew. "At all?" she asked.

"At all," Hammered Silver confirmed. "For now. We may revisit the topic in a year."

A Finger Pointing nodded stiffly, agreed, and scheduled the next lunch date.

✩

The walk home was slow; any faster, and she feared that she might stumble.

Beholden walked with her paws stuffed into the pockets of her hoodie, mostly looking down to her feet as they trudged along the sidewalk, while A Finger Pointing walked with her arm looped through her partner's, trusting the skunk to get them both home.

She needed it. The world had indeed stopped making sense, as though seen in watercolors, too much pigment on canvas. The sound of their footsteps on gravel and concrete and grass was a fine grit within her ears. The sound of the door opening, the feeling of the couch beneath her, the colors of Motes's paintings on the wall, each was too much.

There was panic, there, yes—there was dissociation, derealization, depersonalization—panic about the events, panic about Dry Grass and Motes and herself and Beholden, but there was also exhaustion. There was also the knock-on effects of a fit of play some years back, all welling up within her.

In that fit of play, that bout of instance artistry decades prior, one of her up-tree instances—two degrees up, a fork of a fork—started to crash. Before they did so completely, however, they managed to quit, to merge back down. Her immediate up-tree, another instance of ever-curious her, accepted the merge blithely. After all, when else would she ever know what a crash felt like without crashing herself?

Nothing happened. It was strange, yes. It was weird and confusing and uncomfortable, but it did not hurt, it did not leave that instance of her affected in any apparent way. Just a pile of jumbled memories slowly seeping in between the ones she had made, herself.

And so, A Finger Pointing accepted her up-tree's merge just as blithely.

The effects were both subtle and dramatic.

They were subtle because there was was no sudden incapacitation, no torturous existence that left her craving non-existence. They were subtle because they left her with a life so much like the one she had, but for the fact that her sensorium and sense of self had been severed, separated. *That* was the drama.

This was the dissociation. This was the derealization. This was the world around her ceasing to make sense, as though in a dream. As though in a dream because she *did* live in a dream, did she not? She lived in the consensual dream that was the System, yes? It was hyper-dreaming, then, it was understanding a dream within a dream.

It was like the System before the dream had been made consensual. It was like what image or audio or video transfers had been attempted before the introduction of AVEC, all blurry, all smudged, all almost-but-not-quite what they were, what they were meant to be.

It was having a conversation with a dear one when tired, when one's attention drifted, and then trying to repeat the words that you had almost but not quite heard. It was looking at a scene and remembering that you were standing on a beach a moment ago, and yet being unable to tell water from shore, from sand. It was looking at your partner and not recognizing their face, not recognizing what a face *was*.

It was pain, but she could not tell where or what kind or even if it was pain at all. It was vertigo. It was no up, no down.

It was curling in the corner in a fetal position because to do aught else was to risk falling over and breaking a limb.

She wished dearly that she could do so now.

✵

The first time Motes called A Finger Pointing 'mom', there had been a conversation, full of various confusions and hurts, inquiries and boundaries, tears and tears and tears. Both came to an agreement that this was not comfortable. Not now. Not yet.

These optics they must consider, this awful taboo, they spoke of intraclade relationships in terms of incest, and now here was her Motes reifying this abstract concept of family by calling her 'mom'! Such language had ever been used as a weapon against her and her Beholden, and it was not yet time to reclaim that.

It built up a false equivalence within all three of them. It allowed them to consider this taboo as applying to all relationships within a clade beyond simple community, simple friend-ship; all those big-R Relationships like those of A Finger Point-ing and Beholden, and like those of Motes with the two of them were of equal dire import. This desire for such family to be con-strained to a private setting must apply to all types of family dynamics, yes?

A year later—for what is a year to a cladist?—Motes did it again, and this time she asked first, and permission was granted to see how it felt. It was still quite uncomfortable, but perhaps there was joy to be found. Perhaps there were expectations and standards and trust that could be built up, refinements to be made. Not mother, no, but perhaps 'ma' was alright. Not daugh-ter, no, but what of *dóttir?* What of 'Ma' and 'Dot'?

"Beholden and I are still smarting because we must se-quester our affection for one another in private. That is why I have been hesitant to take on the caregiver role that you have sought from me," A Finger Pointing had said during that quiet night's conversation, skunklet curled beside her on the couch, getting pets. "But I do care for you, do I not? I do feel like a sort of matron amidst the fifth stanza, do I not? Perhaps it is time I reconsidered my aversion to such language. Perhaps it is time I considered reclamation. After all, everything I have done has been so that you can live in peace. Are you living in peace, Motes? Are you at peace when you must restrain your feelings for me for reasons neither of us particularly care for?"

And so, as it had been with each of Motes's tentative explo-rations and gentle testing of mutable boundaries, this became a thing that was okay at home, okay in limited doses, okay for a trial period. It was worthy of exploration, for if there was the potential for joy—and everyone deserved such—then perhaps there was some way Motes could be granted such a thing.

This private setting, this iterative context, this ongoing play allowed for growth and change.

There was still soreness, of course. There was soreness that A Finger Pointing and her Beholden still had to deal with the optics, that it was still not permissible for this reason or that for them to kiss in public, for them to share their I-love-yous where others might witness that joy. There was still soreness that such soreness affected Motes.

And so it remained largely at home, at home with the three of them and at home in the neighborhood that was slowly building up around them. It remained a secret, but, like A Finger Pointing and Beholden's relationship, it remained an open one. The quiet of the secret allowed them live to their fullest, and the openness allowed them to share joy where they felt safe doing so.

Six months later: another letter. Another statement of distaste, and with it, a firm boundary. There was to be no further discussion of And We Are The Motes In The Stage-Lights from thence forth. Period.

⁂

"I am tired, Beholden."

"I know, love," the skunk said, sitting beside her on the couch and dreaming up a glass of water for her.

She could still comprehend, at least, and could still see Beholden there beside her, a look of tired concern painted on her face.

"Do you need anything else?"

She shook her head and carefully sipped her water. "Nothing in particular, no, though if you could stay here for a little while, I would appreciate that."

"Do not be ridiculous," Beholden said with a wan smile. "Like I would ever fucking leave. I *am* going to send a fork to go check on Dot, though."

"Please do so, yes."

A second instance of Beholden appeared to the other side of her, pushing herself up and padding to go poke her head into Motes's room, then quitting from there. "She is asleep still, I think, or close enough. She has not moved."

A Finger Pointing sighed. "I suppose she would not have, no." She rolled her head to the side to glance at her partner, saying, "I have an idea for what to do, but I am worried about what it will mean."

" 'What it will mean'? Not what it will accomplish?"

"Yes. I do not think that you will like it, but I think it will accomplish much of what Waking World said. It will get her to just leave us alone. To leave Motes and Dry Grass be."

Beholden nodded slowly. "That is good, then."

"It will just mean a bit of a compromise on my morals." She paused, organizing her thoughts. "It will mean letting some of this hurt through. It will mean letting Hammered Silver get to me—just a little bit—so that she can feel a little bit of a victory and hold onto that instead of us. It is a compromise."

The skunk bridled. "You are right. I do not like it at *all*. That is a shitty fucking compromise."

She chuckled drily, took another sip of water. "To be fair, my muse, neither do I, but if it gets her to fuck off for good, then so be it."

⭐

An end to a friendship with a person is not the end of knowing that person. An end to a friendship can be sudden or gradual. It can be the type of thing that happens in one fell swoop: an argument, perhaps, or a disappearance. It can be the type of thing that takes months and years and decades: a drifting apart, perhaps, or a series of slow decisions. It can be both: an inflection point is reached and neither realizes it until down the line and, oh, perhaps it had ended long ago.

A Finger Pointing was not sure when it was that her friendship with Hammered Silver *actually* died, because there were so many points at which it *could have* died that it was hard to pick just one. There were so many letters, now all stored in a single exo so that they would not simply live within her actual memory at all times, and each of those could have been the end of a friendship as easily as any other.

There was still that point of realization, though. There was that point when she realized that she had long ago ceased to be Hammered Silver's friend, had long ago become merely her co-cladist, some obligation to be followed up upon out of a tired sense of formality or information gathering over friendship-colored lunches.

They were friendship colored because that was the tinted glass that A Finger Pointing held before her eyes. She viewed the world with friendship, with the joy of joy itself. She looked at all times through a gel—one of those transparent, colored sheets used to tint a stage-light—colored with friendship, colored by joy.

It was not a pair of rose-colored glasses. She was not burying her head in the sand to avoid some unpleasant facts. She was as realistic as ever she had been, as Sasha/Michelle had been before her and Michelle Hadje before that.

It was an expectation of herself and others. It was a standard to which she and others were held. It was a trust that others would aim for joy and friendship as she did.

And thus it was an expectation one might fall short of. It was a standard one might not reach. It was a trust that could be breached.

At some point in the past—there were so many admonitions against joy that she could choose from!—A Finger Pointing's friendship with Hammered Silver came to an end. The most visible of these was perhaps when Sasha became which she was, back when True Name had been all but assassinated, back when she had no choice but to change her very identity and become something new, something more. That was when Hammered Silver had, spurred by In Dreams, taken the drastic measure of cutting off not just Sasha herself, but the entirety of the eighth stanza for their politicking, the first for their spying, and part of the ninth for some mere association. All of those, yes, as well as the entirety of the fifth stanza for, as she had said in as many words, their perfidy.

For the rest of the fifth stanza also bore this expectation, this standard, this trust that there was within all people something worth friendship, some kernel of joy, and none of them shunned Sasha, either. They were all precisely as guilty as the rest of the eighth stanza for their support.

Cutting contact is one hell of a way to end a friendship, yes?

But no, the end of their friendship had almost certainly come far earlier. Decades earlier.

At some point back in the early 2100s, Motes had begun exploring this role of the babiest Odist of the fifth stanza—in her twenties, sure, but a being built entirely out of play. A note arrived.

At some point back in the late 2100s, Motes had begun exploring this form of childhood—no one's child in particular, sure, and everyone's, but a being built entirely out of play. A note arrived.

And at some point back in the late 2200s, Motes had begun exploring the concept of family. She moved in with A Finger Pointing and Beholden, and the longer she stayed, the more she fell in love with them as her guardians and the more they fell in love with her as their charge.

For this was true of all of her up-trees, and for much of Au Lieu Du Rêve besides. Going years back, back even to the late 2100s, this reveling in play that Motes brought to the fifth stanza had built in A Finger Pointing a sense of her place in the order: her role was a maternal one. A reveling in care, in the type of friendship that flowered in a particular dynamic.

She was their matron, in a way. She was their protector. She shielded them as best she could from the politics that so much of their cocladists were engaging in throughout the rest of the System. "But that is my job," she reasoned aloud when she became more open about this protection. "That is why we have an administrator for Au Lieu Du Rêve, yes? Someone has to deal with the politics of running a theatre, yes?"

But then, some time back around systime 182, back around the time the clocks ticked over to 2306, back around the time Michelle/Sasha had summoned them all to her field to merge centuries of memory and then quit—perished—Hammered Silver sent one of her longest letters yet. It was in some ways a screed. It was beyond simply admonition, note, or missive. It was an epistle, some general letter intended to be a point of instruction not just to her but to the world as a whole.

The screed—well worth embodying as a physical letter if only to be torn up, ripped to shreds, burnt to ash, soaked with tears to douse the fire, ground into a paint, and used to spell out anger and despair—laid out in nigh-unintelligible detail all of the ways in which she and hers had fallen short.

Motes had existed. She had tested the limits and found them flexible. She had found the boundaries negotiable. She had poked her nose out into the world and found it largely amenable to her existence. She had lived her life in play. She had played as a child and played as an adult. She had gone down slides and been bitten during sex and died on-stage and off, all countless times.

All of these were unacceptable. All of these had led to letters and notes of their own. All were rehashed through paragraph after paragraph of spiny invective.

But a full half of the letter was devoted to a particular combination of particular topics that had apparently struck Hammered Silver as particularly worthy of ire: Motes had started calling A Finger Pointing 'Ma' and A Finger Pointing had started calling Motes 'Dot'. Two syllables worthy of an essay-length diatribe, for if A Finger Pointing and Beholden had bought into the taboo in their own way, accepted it as the way of the world for so long, Hammered Silver had wrapped herself up in it most securely.

How dare she, Hammered Silver cried—and with such a loss as that of Sasha/Michelle, she truly sobbed. How dare she test the clade's position in this most precarious life time and again by doing this awful, awful thing. On and on and on.

She proved their fears accurate, in her own unkind way.

And so, at that point, their friendship ended. They went a year without meeting, and when next they scheduled a coffee date, they spoke hardly at all. They made their goodbyes wordless. The next meeting was similarly silent.

There was no more love between them. The trust had been broken. They met perhaps once a year to keep tabs on each other. They met to ensure that the other was not living outside the bounds of society in some abhorrent way. They met to spy on each other.

That was the time their friendship died, the moment A Finger Pointing received that letter, the one that she tore up and burned to ash, cried over and then, determined, used the paint of which to spell out renewed love for those who remained in her life.

✩

The dissociation had before long defined her life, her existence.

It had dampened her hedonism. It had put a stopper on so much of her wild enthusiasm and had led her to so often asking Beholden to take her home when she had so often before outlasted the skunk on their outings. Whereas before she had dwelt in even the excesses of hedonism until she overflowed and locked herself away from it, a self-harm by omission, she now dwelt in the quietudes of hedonism until she overflowed and threw herself with abandon into wildnesses, a self-harm by overindulgence.

The dissociation, derealization, depersonalization had defined her in her play and, perhaps more painfully, in her care. Here she was, sat on the couch and staring unseeing toward the kitchen, having had to step away from a meeting of care, unable to engage. Here she was, unable to help—never mind that there may not be anything she *could* do to help right now—until her sense of self recohered, until she could return to that care.

Once she had had her water, and then a simple drink mixed by Beholden, and spent an hour resting once the wave of dissociation had started to roll back out, A Finger Pointing stood and walked to the back patio, out where the concrete ended in a sharp seam and the wild grass of the field threatened to tickle at her ankles, were it not for socks and slacks.

She forked, and her new instance moved to stand facing her. When she nodded, the instance opened a simplex sensorium message to Hammered Silver. It was essentially a recording of whatever the instance saw and heard that would be sent when she was finished.

"Memory Is A Mirror Of Hammered Silver," she began, bowing toward her recording instance. "I will not apologize for breaking our silence, but I will allow it to fall over us once more after I am finished with this message. This is simply too important for me to leave unsaid.

"The letters that you have sent to me, Dry Grass, and Motes have left in their wake a pain that I cannot adequately describe. Motes was pushed almost immediately into overflowing, leaving her all but catatonic and unable to interact with the world." She laughed, letting the exhaustion she felt show through along with the very real pain. "Hell, I wish that I could do the same right now, myself."

She sighed, took a moment to reclaim her calm, and continued from there. "I understand that we have irreconcilable differences of opinion on this. I will not attempt to sway you, just as I know that you will not attempt to sway me. That is the point of this no-contact order that you have levied, broken, and then reinforced."

She cursed herself mentally for that 'broken', a little bit of her anger showing through. She only hoped that it came across as yet more pain. She did not want this to turn into a fight.

"I will follow that order to the best of my abilities going forward, but you must understand that you have wounded us, well and truly." She bowed once more before saying, "I will expect no reply," and then falling silent.

Her recording instance sighed once the message was sent and then quit.

With that done, she turned to face out to the prairie, and spent a few minutes just enjoying a little bit of stillness, a little bit of quiet. The air was just on the cool side of perfect. There was the smell of rain. The sky was gray without being bruised.

And then, with a small ping of a notification, an envelope blipped into being at eye level and fluttered down to the ground before her.

"Of course," she mumbled, bending down to pick it up. Sure enough, it bore the expected handwriting, the expected address.

> **To:** Time Is A Finger Pointing At Itself of the Ode clade **(EYES-ONLY)**
> **From:** Memory Is A Mirror Of Hammered Silver of the Ode clade
> **On:** systime 238+292
>
> Time Is A Finger Pointing At Itself,
>
> I have received your message. I appreciate your acknowledgment that you will not change my mind. I hope that you consider that this is because there is a correct and incorrect way of thinking about these issues.
>
> May the pain be instructive, and may the silence between our stanzas be complete.
>
> Memory Is A Mirror Of Hammered Silver

She read the letter through twice and then committed it to her long-running exocortex and destroyed the original.

"What a fucking bitch," she muttered to herself as she turned to return inside.

At least it had worked.

A simple dinner. A few glasses of wine. A quiet evening saying nothing as she lounged with her head on Beholden's lap while the skunk worked. Simple pleasures as she mulled over the day and its varied traumas.

There was so much more she wished she had done. There was so much more she wished she *could* have done. Perhaps there was nothing more available to her, no further tasks before her to address in order to make Motes more comfortable or Dry Grass's life easier, but all the same, the drive to care itched. It grated up against her inability to engage further, thanks to her sense of self already being stretched taut, thanks to that dissociation preventing her from being more earnestly herself.

As darkness fell, as they planned on bed, she checked up on Motes for herself.

The skunk lay tightly curled beneath her covers, a pillow held tightly in her arms, eyes clenched tightly shut. She was tempted to stand there for a few minutes, simply watching her charge, her Dot, sleep.

Or...not sleep, but withdraw from the waking world.

Better to show what she could. She stepped quietly into the room and climbed up onto Motes's bed with her, curling behind her and draping an arm across the little skunk.

"I love you, Dot," she mumbled, burying her face against the back of her neck. "I am sorry."

There was more she could say—so much more—but for some reason, words failed her after that. Words and will both failed her, and so she simply lay there with Motes, replying to Beholden's gentle, inquiring ping with a soothing one of her own. She had told Motes that she loved her, as she never tired of doing so, and that was enough.

She lay there until she felt her *dóttir* slowly relax beneath her arm, heard her breathing slow, and then for a while after.

Beholden — 2362

# 8

Beholden never quite understood play.

She *played,* that was for sure. She played with her music, her sound design. She played with people's voices, recording them for later and slicing them up into bits and bites, rebuilding them into some work of eerie or jittery or calming beauty. She played with the sounds around her house, her studio, the whole of the world. She played with acoustics. She played with spaces. She played with echoes and reverberations and dead-zones and cones of silence. She played with soundscapes and world-soundtracks.

She hummed and sang. She played the piano, the drums, the guitar. She played the clarinet badly and the flute worse. She played with A Finger Pointing, their own little jazz trio, their own little big band. She played with her friends, jam session after jam session after jam session. She played her own sets, forking countless times over to play at however many clubs or venues. She played at The Party—several instances thereof!—running now for the last century and a half, a party that never ceased, attendees sleeping wherever: in beds or where they had fallen, with each other, alone. Beholden To The Flow Of The Crowds existed for a reason, yes?

She played as she danced. She played with others, dragging them home for a one-night stand, a few-nights' fling, a relationship that lasted a month or two, but so rarely any longer.

And she played with Motes, too. She really did! She played with her little Dot, tickling her until she said she was going to be sick, or pretending to pick her up by the ears as the skunklet clutched at her forearms. She played dead for Motes when she grew too exhausted to keep up. She lay there, on the floor, eyes closed, breathing turned off, while her charge scampered around, leaping over her, triumphant, hollering about victories, or wept over her unalive-yet-still-souled body at the tragedy— oh, woe! Such tragedy!—of a fallen comrade. Less mother than cool stepdad, she played with her kid.

But she did not understand it. She did not really get it. She rarely thought about it, but when she did, it was more baffling than it was natural.

Beholden was not stupid. She was not an idiot. She could conceptualize things around her, and, as in all the many ways the rest of the clade was, she was wickedly intelligent in her own area of hyperfixation, hyperspecialization. When it came to emotions, though, when it came to instincts and base responses, she could not quite understand. It was not her fixation, her specialization.

She did not really know why she played, because she did not really *care* to know why.

She did not know why she loved or Motes. She did not know why she loved so few others. She did not know why she felt such devotion to her boss—"not your boss" the common refrain—and her Dot in a way that she could not muster for anyone else. She never bothered to question why.

She did not know why she rose so quickly to anger. She did not know why she and Motes fought at times. She did not know why she got so mad when she saw Motes die on stage. She did not know why, when she and Slow Hours fought—usually about Motes's various deaths—it hurt so much. She shied away from ever trying to figure out why.

She just knew that she played, that she loved, and that she got stuck in her big feelings.

And so when she found Motes huddled in the middle of her studio, all but curled into a ball as she crouched on the floor, when she found her bloodied, beat up, Beholden panicked. She kept it together long enough to help the little skunk to her room, to fork, to bed. She held herself in one piece as she told Motes time and again that she loved her. She held the panic at bay until she made her way to her studio, locked the completely sound-proof door, and crumpled to the ground, screaming and wailing and sobbing. She tore holes in the couch cushions with her claws. She ripped acoustic foam from the walls. She threw the table hard enough to shatter it.

And then, when sobs settled into simple tears and not great, heaving things, she waved her paw to unwind the tantrum. She brought into being a glass of water to set on the once more intact table, sat down on the un-torn couch, and moaned through her tears, letting the replaced acoustic foam absorb her despair.

When she was next able to speak, she began a sensorium message to A Finger Pointing. *"Dot is overflowing, love. She–"*

*"I know,"* her partner interrupted. *"I am here."*

Quelling her shame, she straightened herself up as best she

could, deciding not to fork away the mussed up fur or tear-stains on her cheeks, letting some of that trauma show for reasons she could not explain—validation, perhaps?—and stepped back out of her studio to find A Finger Pointing pacing back and forth in the living room.

"I came as soon as- oh, Beholden..." Her cocladist's shoulders slumped as she trailed off, putting a halt to her pacing so that she could wrap the skunk up in a hug. "Are you okay, my dear?"

Despite the stinging of new tears in her eyes, she nodded. "Not particularly, but I am here. How did you know that Motes was overflowing?"

A Finger Pointing hesitated, frowned, and pulled a letter from her pocket, handing it over to the skunk. "This. I did not *know* that Dot was overflowing until I got here and saw her door shut tight. I was not at all surprised when you told me."

As Beholden read through the letter, her lips curled up into a snarl, and she could feel a low growl build in her chest. " 'I expect better'!" she muttered darkly, stamping her foot. "Jesus *fucking* Christ. 'Grounded in reality' indeed."

Smiling humorlessly, A Finger Pointing nodded toward the paper in her paws. "I am assuming that this mention of a letter is what took Motes down."

"Took her down?" Beholden cried, then quickly tamped down the flare of anger, returning the letter to her partner. "She was covered in blood when I checked on her. Someone must have hit her hard enough to give her a bloody nose. She was all scraped up."

A Finger Pointing froze, face drained of color, then nodded slowly. "Did you get her cleaned up?"

"Yeah, I brought her to enough to get her to fork into her PJs, but she is out hard right now in bed."

"Thank you, my muse. I had assumed the last bit, at least, and have left her be. I did not wish to add to her stress at the moment."

Beholden nodded. "What do we do?"

"Protect our own," came the immediate answer. "Protect ourselves. Protect our Dot."

And so they did. They made their calls. They brought Dry Grass into the fold as officially as they saw fit, providing her with a house. They set up a gentle watch on Motes, set up alerts throughout the house for when her door opened from the inside, for when the bar or kitchen were entered by her. They sought out Slow Hours for a meeting asking for her premonitions, such as they were. They sought out Sasha for a meeting to confirm that there were no existential threats. They sought out Waking World for a meeting to get a better sense of Hammered Silver's intentions.

All the while, Beholden did her best to remain calm, or to at least push down expressions of overwhelming emotions. There were walks. Many walks. Many excuses to step away to the auditorium or to get fresh air or stretch her legs.

She went always alone on her walks, pacing out along the deer trails or walking the loop of the neighborhood time and again or poking her way among the seats and catwalks of the auditorium.

Or tried to go alone, as always there was someone willing to go with her, asking gently if she needed company, even if that company was silent, or if she needed instead to talk. Slow Hours volunteered. Unbidden volunteered. A Finger Pointing, having spent so many years, so many decades with her, did not volunteer, but did look after her with a mix of worry and understanding in her face.

The only time she accepted the company was when Dry Grass, fresh out of her meeting with Sasha, did not so much volunteer as, wiping freshly-shed tears from her face, ask Beholden if they could go for a walk together so that she could talk. That Beholden had already slipped on her hoodie, had already drank a glass of water, was already heading towards the door suggested that this was a form of volunteering, but Dry Grass certainly deserved as much as anyone the chance to talk through the position she had found herself in, so Beholden reluctantly said yes.

The two walked in silence, both looking down at the sidewalk as it passed beneath their feet, both processing in their own way.

"Hey, uh," Beholden said at last once they had made it halfway through the neighborhood, halfway around the usual loop. "Are you okay? I mean, things are awful, but are you feeling okay?"

Dry Grass started at the sudden intrusion of words, smiling sheepishly over to the skunk. "I mean, no. Yes, in a way, but also no."

Beholden smiled wryly. "Do you think you could unpack that for me?"

She laughed. "Right, sorry. I am a bit all over the place at the moment." She took a deep breath before continuing. "No, I am not okay. I do not even like Hammered Silver, nor do I– *did* I speak with many of the others in my stanza with any frequency, but Hammered Silver stabbed me all the same. It hurts to have someone hate me so much, never mind someone who is also in many ways me."

"And the 'yes' part?"

The answer was a long time coming. "I feel vindicated," Dry Grass said at last. "I feel validated that my estimate of Hammered Silver was correct. She is worse than I thought, maybe, but at least I was not wrong, yes?"

Beholden snorted. "Wrong in the correct direction."

She nodded, smiling as her gaze drifted out into the neighborhood, over at the playground in the central area. "And yes because I am finding out in a very real way that there are still people on my side, that I still have friends. I still get to spend time with you and A Finger Pointing, and I still get to spend time with Motes. I just feel bad that she wound up at the center of this."

"I do too," the skunk mumbled. "I love that kid. I say it as often as I can, but I always worry that I am not as good at showing it as I could be."

Dry Grass gently nudged her across the street, aiming for the playground and saying as she did so, "I think that is something that every parent worries about."

"I do not know that I am—"

"No, no, I get it," she said, taking a seat on one of the swings. "I know that it is complicated. It is easier for some of us, but even my stanza, even the ones who leaned hard into feelings of motherhood still struggle with what it means to call someone like Motes *their* child. Not just a child, but theirs. You do feel some of that sense of parenthood, though, do you not?"

"Oh, definitely," Beholden answered without hesitation, claiming a swing beside Dry Grass's. "She is my Dot, I am her Bee. It took me a long time to get to this point, though, and even still, it feels weird at times."

"I am curious how, if you are open to sharing."

She shrugged. "Sure, though I also want to know why you are curious about this in particular."

Dry Grass smiled, shrugged as well. "Something to talk about that is not my down-tree being a terrible fucking person."

Beholden barked a laugh. "Okay, yeah, that is fair." She scuffed a paw against the gravel, thinking. "It was mostly just hard for me to wrap my head around, I guess. I have some of those same desires in me as your whole stanza does, but they were always minimized and pushed to the side. Even boss has way more than I do, right? Like, it is her job to take care of things. She is not really the boss of Au Lieu Du Rêve, she is its mom."

Holding onto the chains of the swing and nudging herself back a meter or so with her feet, Dry Grass nodded. "I can see that, yes. It is like how I headed into systech stuff because I cared for the System." She smiled faintly. "I was Lagrange's mom."

The skunk nodded. "Yeah, like that. I just have way less of that in me than either you or A Finger Pointing. You are both way better at this than I am. Dot means a lot to me. A whole lot. That we have to have a systech on staff to kick her into forking whenever she dies on stage just kills me. It breaks my heart whenever I see that."

Dry Grass winced. "Me too. I will not show up to a performance if I know that will happen."

"Really? Shit. I am sorry. At least I am not alone in that," Beholden mumbled, nudging herself to start swinging as well. "It is moments like those when I feel most like she is my kid, though. I feel that family dynamic most when she is at risk, you know? When Slow Hours and I argue about that sort of thing, that is when I feel most protective of her, like my sister is doing something bad to my kid."

"Was it always like that?" Dry Grass asked. "Did you always feel that?

She hesitated, simply letting the swing carry her for a few moments. "I do not know. I was really caught off guard when she started calling A Finger Pointing 'Ma'. I mean, so was A Finger Pointing, but that had a lot of implications for me, too, did it not? I was suddenly her mom's wife, right? Or at least partner."

Dry Grass nodded.

"So it took me a lot of getting used to." She hesitated, looked down to the gravel as she kicked a foot through it. "I am a little ashamed to say that I backed off from her for a while when she did that. I took a lot of walks like this or went out to clubs on my own to...well, to not be around her. I loved her even then, but it felt like too much. 'Bee' is a compromise that felt on the edge of comfort at the time, though now it feels really good when she calls me that. She was so patient with me." Drawing her attention back to Dry Grass, she smiled, adding, "She calls you 'Ma 2.0'; did you know that?"

Dry Grass blinked, then burst out in laughter, laughing until once more the tears flowed down her cheeks, until she sobbed, holding herself still on her swing with feet planted firmly on the ground.

Beholden waited in silence. She knew well the mechanics of a hysterical laugh-cry—she had at one point recorded A Finger Pointing falling into such and chopped it into little slivers of half-recognizable samples and haunted an entire album with it, so beautiful had she found it—and while her and Dry Grass's relationship did not include a whole lot of hugging, she still nudged herself to the side far enough to rub at her cocladist's shoulder until the tears once more slowed and she was once more able to breathe but for a few aftershocks of chuckling.

"Sorry, Beholden," Dry Grass said, once she was able. "I am a little fucked up still, I think."

She chuckled. "I mean, this is a pretty fucked situation, my dear. I would be surprised if you were not."

They both settled into swinging in silence once more, just a gentle rocking back and forth to calm down and enjoy time away from so much stress before it would doubtless ramp up once more when Waking World was set to visit after lunch.

"Hey, Beholden?"

"Mm?"

"Can you tell me something good?" Dry Grass sighed, gaze drifting out over nothing in particular. "Just a good memory about Motes or the fifth stanza or whatever. Something to make this all feel a bit more worthwhile."

Beholden let her swinging come to a stop as she thought back across the years, hunting for something that might fit. Finally, she said, "One year, boss got Motes this harness that wrapped all the way around her torso and around her thighs like a climbing harness or something. It let us carry her around like a briefcase."

Dry Grass laughed. "Oh god, I cannot imagine."

Grinning, the skunk continued, "That was fun enough, but what we would use it for was, on summer days, we would lift her up, give her a good heave-ho and toss her into the pool. She would laugh so hard that she would have a hard time swimming and kept swallowing too much pool water. When it was winter, we would have it snow a bunch in one spot-" She pointed over toward a spot by the slide. "-and toss her into it, or let her go down the slide directly into the snow bank. We should dig it out again soon. When she is better, I mean."

"I am absolutely going to do that if you all are comfortable."

Beholden laughed. "To her? Or as yourself?"

"Oh, to her!" she said, smirking. "Though who knows, maybe I would give the slide version a go, myself."

The conversation of good things continued—Motes designing the playground; the slide that Warmth In Fire, Serene, and In The Wind designed that led to a hidden world of ghostly forests if you believed it would; Warmth In Fire designing the chalk lines that followed the two of them as they ran around; A Finger Pointing and Beholden sitting on the stoop of their home to watch the sun set while little ones played in the grass—until they grew weary of the swings digging into their backsides and hunger started tugging them back toward home and what joys they had built began to fade in the face of the immediate past.

With each step, a bit of color once more seeped from the world and a bit more worry once more gnawed at Beholden's gut.

Lunch, despite being a sauce served over rice, was all the same dry and ashen in her mouth as she struggled with so many swirling feelings, so many spiraling thoughts around what had happened.

Still, she managed to clean her plate, managed to straighten herself up for the meeting with Waking World, managed to only yell at him a little bit. She managed as best she could as they did their best to learn what paths forward they had.

She tamped down her emotions throughout, press-fit them into place within her so that they would not spill over into the world around her, bottled them up, wrote a label on the jar, and set it on a shelf high in her mind to deal with later, right next to all of the other jars about which she had promised the same.

She had to, at least for now, at least for the time being. She would someday need to reckon with the person that she had built herself up into. She would need to deal with all of the compromises that she had made in order to be Beholden. She was Beholden To The Heat Of The Lamps! Sound and music director for the troupe! She was lead sound tech! This was the cost of engaging so closely with what had once been her dearest friend's specialty. Michelle acted, and later taught. AwDae was the sound engineer. This was the price she paid for being Au Lieu Du Rêve's very own AwDae. While the others within the stanza, within the clade, may dance with em as they moved through the System, she, of all them, was perhaps one of the most entangled with em. It was Beholden who was with AwDae on her quiet walks, Beholden who was with AwDae, drunk under the stars, Beholden who was with AwDae when she was working. Or playing. Or crying. Or laughing. Or indulging. She could never escape em, try as she might, and so, from time to time, a woman needed a break from grief.

It was her fragility, and the only way she knew to reinforce herself was through setting such emotions aside. She would need to confront that—that and so many other things—but not just yet, not with so much before her.

And so, when A Finger Pointing stood, wobbled, and requested that she take her home, Beholden immediately stood with her and gently guided her from the library and back to the neighborhood. She let her partner hold onto her to the extent that she was comfortable, rather than the other way around, trusting that she would take only what touch she needed lest she get yet more overwhelmed.

She knew well by now the ways in which A Finger Pointing had changed over the years, about how the crash had affected her.

She knew well because she had seen the exhaustion or fear or slackness in her partner's face when the dissociation would crawl over her, insidious, had heard how she would turn down her sensorium almost all the way just to survive those moments.

She knew well because she had heard A Finger Pointing fall as the world ceased to make sense to her and vertigo rose like bile, had heard the shout of surprise as she tumbled from a catwalk where she had been placing lights, had heard the thud-crunch of her hitting the stage twenty feet below and the note of dreamy confusion in her voice when she realized, "Oh, I am *quite* broken," the tired frustration as she forked herself whole.

So she set her mind to caring for her love. It was as she had always done. It was as she must do. If the crash had shaped the way that A Finger Pointing moved through the world, the way she danced with those around her, so too had it shaped Beholden and her path forward. Even if she did not know it at first, even if her partner had only explained it after the fall, it had shaped the both of their lives and the life of their *dóttir*, brought them in-sensibly closer together over the years to where they were now: a family true.

She pressed those emotions down and instead lingered on love. She lingered on her devotion to A Finger Pointing. She lin-gered on her protectiveness of her charge, her Dot, the child she so often insisted was not her own and yet so often referred to as her kid. She lingered on those good memories as best she could to keep the very air from tasting astringent, to push away the feeling of desiccating sand gritting between her teeth.

Once A Finger Pointing was settled at home and Motes had been checked on, once the message had been sent to Hammered Silver and they had eaten and settled down on the couch for the night to rest, to at least pretend to work, only then, did Beholden very carefully open the jarred emotions from earlier, delicately withdrawing them one by one and laying them out before herself in her mind. She did not touch them, hot as they were. She used tweezers or tongs or perhaps chopsticks to lift them free, nudge them to lay flat that she might read deeper into them.

And then, exhausted by the day, by the last few days, by worry over her Dot, her *dóttir*, by worry over her boss—"not your boss" the common refrain—she just as carefully replaced all of those emotions, still unprocessed, into their container and once more sealed it tight.

She could not do it, could not push her way into engaging with these feelings, these emotions. Not yet. Not tonight.

Perhaps some day she might.

Motes — 2362

# 9

Motes thought of play.

She thought of all of the play that she had taken part in over the years, all of the games and make believe, all of the jungle-gyms and slides, all of the tag and red-light-green-light and duck-duck-goose, everything going back 276 years, as much as she could remember. She thought of all her toys, from the mound of stuffed animals occupying her bed beside her right now to the awful and cheap RC car she had received on her fifth birthday that worked for that day and that day alone, then never again turned on. She thought of all her friends, from Alexei on the playground the other day—three days ago? Four?—calling out to her as she fell under the spike of panic—all the way back to Frida Couch who she had met in kindergarten, who she had told her parents she was dating in third grade, who had died some years after Michelle had uploaded.

She thought of the way that play defined the Motes that she had become, the way it had shaped the way she interacted with the world, the way it shaped her very form. She thought of how Au Lieu Du Rêve had accepted readily just how well it fit her self-definition. She thought of the family that she had built up around her.

She thought of play as she levered herself out of her bed, looked wearily around her room, the toys and art, the stuffed animals and silly prints on clothing, and then she forked into Big Motes.

She forked into Big Motes and straightened her hair and blouse, set a well-remembered dandelion flower crown atop her head, and made her way out to the rest of the house.

There was silence there, and emptiness. There was the place to herself in the warm sunlight of a late morning, some three days after first she fell on the playground. There was the comfort of familiarity set beside a hollow feeling in her chest.

Adjusting to a view of the world a few feet higher than it had been moments before, a view without a snout, movement without a tail, she made her way to the kitchen and poked around. It did not feel like a day for some sugary cereal, nor the cinnamon-sugar toast that she had always loved. It was a day for coffee and something savory and filling and hot. Perhaps a day for a mimosa.

*An adult breakfast,* a part of her whispered. *Setting aside childish things...*

She shook her head to dispel the lingering thought, one based in overflow rather than her current mood.

And so she pulled out a couple of eggs, a few links of chicken sausage, and a dish of frozen hash browns. On a whim, she also pulled out a few large tortillas and some green chili salsa that she—that much of the clade—remembered fondly from her time back phys-side, back when she lived in the central corridor. She may as well go all out, yes?

The hash browns were the first to go in the pan, laid out in an even layer so that they could crisp up. Two more pans were dreamed up so that she could cook the sausage and eggs meanwhile.

Definitely a morning for a mimosa.

The eggs were fried over easy and the sausage cooked to just this side of burnt so that they offered a pleasant mix of textures, crispy on the outside and chewy on the inside with an indulgent oiliness throughout. These were layered on top of a pile of even crispier hash browns—the kind that shatter beneath a fork when you try to stab them—before the eggs were laid on top and the yolks punctured so that they oozed out over the mess to add a sauce of their own.

A plate laden with two burritos in one hand and mimosa in the other, she made her way to the couch rather than the dining table and settled down with a long, worn-out sigh.

What was missing...? Ah! Coffee.

While there was joy in making her own, she was already down, she was already comfortable, she was already finished with her time in the kitchen, and so she deemed it easier to just wave a steaming mug into being on the low table before her, already dosed with cream and sugar.

She downed half of her mimosa in one go before setting that aside and focusing on her first burrito, each bite topped with a generous spoonful of the salsa until she was left nearly in tears. The rest of the mimosa and a few sips of her coffee, and then the second burrito, similarly doctored.

It was some time later—she did not know how long nor care to check, though her coffee mug was empty—before Beholden and A Finger Pointing returned, talking quietly about lunch. On

seeing her awake and alert, the empty dishes on the table, they both smiled and changed course to settle down on either side of her.

"Glad to see you up and about, Dot," Beholden said, briefly touching her nosetip to Motes's cheek in an affectionate skunk-kiss. "We got the ping that you were, thus lunch here rather than out, but it is nice to see you all the same."

Bookending her with a similar—though far more human—kiss to her other cheek, A Finger Pointing said, "It really is. Are you feeling better, my dear? Please say yes."

Motes laughed and waited until each was finished before returning the cheek kisses to her cocladists. "I am, mostly. I still have a lot on my mind, but I am no longer buried beneath it." She nodded towards the plates, adding, "I already ate before you got here. I am not sorry."

"Nor should you be," A Finger Pointing scoffed. "I would be disappointed if you had not."

"Of course you would be." Her grin softened to a smile. "You really set up the sim to ping you when I woke?"

"Just a few things—your door opening, something being done in the kitchen or at the bar, that sort of thing—so that we would know while we were out."

"She was worried," Beholden stage-whispered. "You should have seen her brighten when she got the notification you were in the kitchen."

"Beholden was *so* worried," A Finger Pointing said, voice bearing all the drama of some overwrought Shakespearean performer. She spoke loudly, pretending as though she had not heard Beholden, that the skunk was not even there. "I do not know if you noticed while you were down and out, my dear, but I swear, that skunk checked on you at *least* once an hour."

"She about started crying," Beholden continued, smirk on her muzzle.

""Beholden, you *know* that she will pull through," I kept saying. "She *always* does." You are stronger than your silly cocladist, Dot, are you not?"

"She was so rude, cutting off a conversation with Sasha mid-sentence and begging to rush us back here, then putting on her most nonchalant act."

Motes laughed as they both scoffed at each other, looping

her arms through each of theirs and slouching down, settling into the comfort of touch and family. "You are both nerds," she murmured. "Thank you for keeping an eye on me."

"Of course, my dear," they said in unison. A Finger Pointing continued, "Motes, did you leave any champagne for the rest of us? I would not say no to a Bellini."

"Another mimosa for me, Beholden," Motes added.

Laughing, the skunk gave her one more of those nose-dot kisses before disentangling herself to see to drinks.

"How are you really, Motes?" A Finger Pointing asked, voice lowered less, it seemed, to keep her words from Beholden than to soften the mood. "We need not talk in detail now, but I do wish to know."

"Okay," she said. "Tender, I guess. Sore, maybe? I am not feeling bad, but I am not yet feeling good. I am feeling like the slightest bump with leave me with a bruise."

A Finger Pointing nodded. "I imagine so. Are you up to speaking about what happened?"

She nodded. "A little bit. I will let you know if I need to bow out."

"Of course." A Finger Pointing took a deep breath, composing herself. "Hammered Silver sent me a letter. She mentioned in it that she had sent you one as well."

Motes wilted.

"Yes, I imagine that is much of why you were left overflowing." When Motes nodded, she continued, "I am sorry, my dear. Is that also why you are Big Motes now?"

The answer was a long time coming, the silence filled with the gentle tink of glasses as Beholden mixed their late lunch cocktails, carrying them carefully back to the couch and handing them out so that she could rejoin.

"Yeah," Motes said at last. "At least, I think so. It was something that I did almost on instinct. I knew I wanted to be Big Motes, or at least that I was not ready to be Little Motes yet. Been thinking about that all morning."

Beholden tasted her drink, nodded appreciatively, then asked, "Have you come to any conclusions?"

"I think so," she said, looking down at her mimosa. Beholden had topped it with a maraschino cherry poked through with a cocktail umbrella. There was a warmth of adoration starting to fill that hollow space in her chest. "I am not going to stop playing, not going to stop being Little Motes, but...but that really fucking hurt, and I need to know what to do with that pain before I reengage with that, you know?"

Letting her free arm dangle over the arm of the couch, glass held by the rim, A Finger Pointing tucked her own cocktail umbrella into Motes's hair behind her ear, adding a wheel of bright pink to the yellow of the dandelions before draping her arm around her shoulder. "That does make sense, yes. That was one of my worries, even: that this would leave you too wounded to reengage with that part of you that has been so important over the years."

Motes shook her head gently so as not to dislodge crown or umbrella.

"Good. You are allowed to be Big Motes for a bit while you process this. You are allowed to hold back on all sorts of interactions. I have noticed a lack of 'Ma' or 'Bee'– no, no. No need to explain, just an observation. These are things that we will miss and then rejoice when they return."

She slouched against A Finger Pointing and hugged around her middle, careful not to spill her drink. "Thank you. I really do appreciate it. I will get there, too, for all of that. Just...not yet. Not quite yet."

Beholden smiled, reached out to brush some of her curls away from her face, added, "Yeah. And if you need us to lay off calling you 'Dot', I am sure–"

"Absolutely not," Motes said, laughing. "I would not have you change your ways just because I am feeling icky for a bit."

"It is an offer, Motes," the skunk chided gently. "Not some weird obligation for us."

Her shoulders slumped and she nodded. "Alright. I think my answer still stands, though. I like it when you call me that, even when I am Big Motes. I do not imagine...well, no. I am *sure* this will not last longer than two weeks. That is the deadline I have given myself to process this."

"Of course, Dot," A Finger Pointing said, tightening her grip in a squeeze before gently nudging her to sit back upright. "With this of all things, I am sure there will be more than enough processing to fill that time. The situation has...resolved itself while you were sleeping, but even that resolution is complicated."

"Oh?"

She nodded. "Are you alright to talk about it? I do not know that even Beholden knows the full extent of what happened."

The skunk shook her head.

Despite the already warm feeling in her belly from the first mimosa, Motes quickly finished her second in a few gulps. "Then sure," she said, laughing at the burp that followed. "Hit me."

Beholden punched her gently on the shoulder before taking her empty glass and setting it on the table in front of them.

The full story of what had happened over the last few days between A Finger Pointing and Hammered Silver was laid bare over the next hour. Not just that, but much of their story going back into the past as well; she even, at one point, dreamed up a stack of all 98 letters she had received over the years, totaling nearly 300 pages.

Both Beholden and Motes were left with more than a few questions. Over the last few years, their down-tree instance had opened up more and more about how much she had shielded the stanza from the political machinations of the rest of the clade around them, all of the ways in which she had strove to protect them, for better or for worse, and yet more of this became clear as she spoke about all of the fuss that Hammered Silver had made over the years.

When she finished and all questions had been answered or deferred, they fell into silence for a long few minutes, the three of them just digesting the last few days each in their own way.

Finally, Motes huffed and flopped back against the couch. "What a fucking bitch."

"Dot, language," Beholden scolded.

"Fuck fuck fuck," she said, grinning wildly. "Bitch bitch bitch! You can yell at Little Motes~"

"No, she is right, my muse," A Finger Pointing said. "Fucking bitch."

"Well, okay, no disputes there," Beholden said, waving away the three glasses. "What is on your plate next, Motes?"

She shrugged. "Well, I pinged Miss Genet, so we are going to meet later."

"Therapy!" A Finger Pointing exclaimed, waving a hand at nothing in particular. "What a lovely idea."

"After all that?" Beholden said, smirking. "I am surprised that you have not already scheduled something."

"I am so dreadfully busy, Beholden. You know that."

"You spent yesterday afternoon lounging in the auditorium trying every kind of kettle corn you could find on the exchange."

She sat up straight, staring at her partner like she was some alien creature, some queer thing too dense to understand the importance of kettle corn. "Yes. Busy."

As A Finger Pointing and Beholden finally got around to whipping up lunch for themselves, the conversation once more fell into comfortable chatter, the sort of banter that so often filed the house, and while, by the time her appointment arrived, Motes had not yet felt comfortable enough to refer to them as 'Ma' and 'Bee', that welcoming sense of family had returned in force, and she felt once more in her comfortable role as their Dot, their *dóttir*.

When the afternoon threatened to slide right into evening, Motes slipped away and left A Finger Pointing and Beholden on the couch, canoodling. Clearly that had taken precedence over whatever they had had planned at the auditorium for the rest of the day. That they had come home for her, for Motes, was the base of that warmth that had grown within her.

She made her way out of the house and wandered to the center of the neighborhood. She left the automatic chalk lines going, letting them be the fuel that propelled her forward, let their flowering shapes fit into this perception of herself as a flower child rather than simply a child, a careful reframing that allowed her to have this thing, this gentle goodness.

The neighborhood formed a lazy semicircle, a 'U' that butted up against an avenue that petered out into the nature of the sim in either direction. Across the street sat the back entrance of the theatre Au Lieu Du Rêve kept for its own community. Just homes and a beloved workplace dropped together into an endless landscape like sugar into so much tea.

In the bowl of the 'U' sat all of the common areas. A pool—one with seats and jets, one that could be a hot tub seating a hundred as easily as it could be an Olympic pool—a few tennis courts for the few—who?—who actually enjoyed the game, a liberal dotting of grills—everyone had a favorite—for cook outs, a lake with a paddle boat, a "community center" which had long ago turned into a movie-theater-*cum*-cuddlepit...

And there, right at the very lowest point of the bowl of the 'U' sat the playground. What was initially intended to be Motes's haunt, hers and her friends', had long ago turned into a place for late-night musings. Thousands and thousands of times over the years, couples or small groups or lone individuals would converge on the swings or the slide and sit in the dark, staring up on the star-speckled sky, the Milky Way glowing bright enough to light one's face beyond even the Moon, even the gold-and-black of the rest of the neighborhood with its sodium vapor lamps and countless darknesses. It was a place for play, yes, and it was often used for such, but it was also a place for couples to work out their problems or groups to chat about everything and nothing or for one to sit alone, drunk, beneath the stars, looking up and feeling good or bad or simply introspective.

It was not dark now.

There, on the swings, sat a child, a girl, looking to be perhaps twelve or thirteen with black hair tied in an unruly ponytail, coppery skin shining in the sun, swaying lazily back and forth as she faced away from Motes. She looked mostly down, skidding the heels of her shoes through the gravel beneath the swings, scooping the pebbles out of the way and then smoothing them back into place with her toes.

Motes moved quietly through the grass—quietly enough that the girl did not notice her—and sat down on the free swing within that segment.

"Hi, Sarah," she said.

"Motes! Hi!" the girl said, then hesitated. "You're Big Motes today. Do you want me to Big Sarah?"

Motes held onto the chains of the swing and gave herself a push with her feet, testing the way she glided through the air for a few feet back, then a few feet forward.

"Motes?"

"Yeah, actually. I think I would like Big Sarah today."

Nodding, Sarah Genet stepped off the swing and summarily disappeared, leaving behind a fork still sitting down. This new instance was far older, looking to be sixty or so years old with salt-and-pepper hair in a much neater ponytail, her skin just as brown and yet fraught with wrinkles, her smile kind and gaze always attentive.

"Is this better?" she asked.

Motes smiled, nodded and gave herself another gentle kick, keeping the same back-and-forth going, the same few feet of earth wafting beneath her feet. "Thanks."

"Of course, Motes. Would you like me to prompt or wait?"

She caught herself in the act of merely shrugging, then shook her head to clear it. "Thanks for asking," she said. After a long moment's thought, she sighed. "I think I would like for you to prompt me today. I do not yet know where to start."

"That's fine," Sarah said gently. "You said in your message that you've just come up from overflowing. Can you tell me about that?"

"Mmhm. Just a few hours ago, actually. Beholden and Pointillist are still back at home after coming to check on me." She smiled down to the ground as it swung beneath her. "They set up alerts around the house so they would know when I was up."

"That's sweet of them."

"It is. I...uh," she trailed off. "The overflow started when I got a letter from within the clade. It really fucked me up. Like, *really* bad."

"And that's why you're Big Motes? Why you didn't say 'Ma'?"

She smirked. "You read me like the Sunday comics," she said, laughing. "Yes."

Sarah smiled in turn, far more gently. "Tell me about this letter, then. Tell me what'd be enough for you to get knocked out of commission."

And so she did. She summarized portions of it, then pulled it up to read the most impactful bits. She talked about the feelings of the month leading up to this, the conversations and the dream. She talked about how she had stopped playing, how it hurt to think of reengaging, how she knew she would but there was work to be done first.

And then, on Sarah's gentle urging, she worked her way backwards. She worked her way back through the months and years before, the feelings that lingered, the various comings-to-terms that she had had over the decades. She talked through and made her own connections, letting Sarah suggest when her voice stumbled to a halt.

"Motes," Sarah said gently. "Tell me why Hammered Silver's opinion matters to you."

Motes snorted. "It should not."

"But it does, doesn't it? A Finger Pointing has addressed it and you're all but guaranteed to not have to deal with this again unless Hammered Silver's gone off the deep end, which it doesn't sound like she has."

She nodded slowly, mulling the question over in her head, brow furrowed.

"Let me split it into two, maybe. First, what about it hurt? Why are you still hurting? And second, who is Hammered Silver to you?"

Motes put her feet down, letting the drag of shoe against gravel slow her to a stop. "Who is she to me? You mean, other than a weirdly invasive aunt who thinks she knows better?" The bitterness in her voice rose, and she was helpless to stop it. "Some old bat who is more concerned about the image of the clade that any—literally *any*—of us living earnestly?"

Sarah raised a brow. "That is absolutely an answer, yes. You still see her as part of the clade?" she asked. "You still see her as an aunt?"

Stymied, she ground her heels down against the gravel beneath the swing.

"I think it's worth digging into, but if you need–"

"No, that is a good point." Motes groaned. That hollow feeling within her chest once more grew, and she squinted her eyes shut. "I guess I do, yeah."

"To which? A part of the clade or aunt?"

"Both."

"Why do you feel she's still a part of the clade to you? That feels like it might be the easier one to answer."

Motes nodded. "Yeah. I guess it just feels like that is something that only the cladist can decide, right? I cannot just say that she is *not* an Odist."

"Hasn't she done that to you and yours, though?"

She furrowed her brow, using her shoe to flatten out the gravel beneath her as she thought. "I do not know that she has, though. She still calls me And We Are The Motes In The Stage-Lights—she was such a bitch about names, actually, 'the one who has named herself Sasha' *every* time—and even if she did not need to, she did write 'of the Ode clade' after my name."

"That's your name, though. Tell me about how that doesn't *feel* like cutting you out of the clade." Sarah smiled gently, adding, "Not that I don't believe you, I just want to understand where you're coming from on this."

"I guess it is that she has not told anyone but her stanza not to talk to me. To us, I mean. Her and In Dreams's stanzas talk to each other. They still talk to the second, third, and fourth. They still talk to What Lives and so on in the ninth. We talk to all of those people, too." She smiled sidelong at Sarah. "So I guess I see where you are going. I do still see her as an aunt because she has not actually said that we are not family—or like a family—she has just cut off contact. She has implied that we *are* still family, but that I did something wrong by...I do not know. Tempting Dry Grass?"

Sarah laughed. "I really was just trying to figure things out, not lead you along, but that's an important connection to make, there. Family members cutting off others in the family is common enough to be a whole area of study. How does it feel to treat the rest of the clade as an extended family, though?"

"That is, like...my whole bit, is it not? I am play-acting the kid. I am method-acting, and Pointillist and Beholden and Slow Hours and everyone is in on it."

"Even Hammered Silver? Even those who *aren't* in on it?" Motes frowned.

"It's okay if you act as though they are," Sarah said. "Or if they become a part of your internal conception of the play. They don't need to be actively in on it if it's an internal representation of your world."

"Right," she mumbled, looking out into the neighborhood and swaying gently from side to side in her swing. "I guess it makes more sense when you talk about family members cutting each other off. If that is a thing that families do with any frequency, then there is no reason for me to not incorporate that."

"'No reason'?" Sarah asked, picking up on the rhythm of Motes's swaying.

"Well, obviously I hate it," she said, laughing. "But if I am going to get shit on like this, then I guess all I can do–"

"'All'?"

Motes snorted. "*One* thing I can do is reclaim it and turn it into a family spat, right?"

Sarah pushed herself to start swinging. "That's what I was getting at, yeah. But tell me more about being Big Motes. You've talked about the family aspect of it, but it sounds like you were thinking about this even before Hammered Silver sent you her letter."

Before she realized what she was doing, Motes was already starting to swing along with Sarah. Back to that movement, back to that little twinge of play. *This* was why she appreciated her therapist, all of these little nudges, all of this meeting her on her terms. After all, had she not appeared at first as a girl a few years older than Little Motes, as she had so many times before? One of those girls who seems infinitely wise to someone younger?

Motes smiled faintly out to the world as it swung beneath and around her. "I do not know that there was anything that spurred on all of the discussions or the dream—though I imagine the dream was a result of all of the thinking that I had been doing leading up to it. It was just on my mind. Maybe I have been doubting myself more of late."

"Doubting how? The last time we talked, you didn't sound like you were doubting yourself. You talked about how everyone had a different nickname for you."

She laughed, feeling earnest joy at the memory. "Dot! Speck! Mote! Kiddo and skunklet and little one," she called out to sky and grass. "Yes, you are right. But I also talked about how I had fallen again into that feeling that maybe my name had played a role in who I had become. Motes, yes? Small, little things that drift across your vision. Microscopic things. I talked about whether the name came first, or the nature, yes?"

"Mmhm. You used Beholden as a counter example."

"I said she should have been in charge of lights," Motes said, still grinning. " 'Beholden to the heat of the lamps'? That has nothing to do with music or sound."

Sarah countered, "And then I pointed out Loss For Images and That It Might Give. 'That it might give the world orders' being primarily a director is pretty on the nose."

"Yeah," she said, sighing as the grin started to fade. "Yeah. There is a mix of both. It does not matter whether or not the name or the nature came first, not in this case. What matters is that it got stuck in my craw, right? I got stuck thinking about it, and then Hammered Silver sent me her stupid letter and it all came to a head."

"Some things are just coincidences."

Motes nodded.

"Hammered Silver sent you the letter because she learned about Dry Grass visiting the fifth stanza. That's not something you had any say over—at least not beyond liking when she visits—and certainly not anything to do with how you were feeling, right?"

She remained silent. She remained silent for a long time, and when the arc of her swing started to slow, she began pumping her legs, working vigorously to get herself swinging as high as she could, swinging to the point where she looked now straight down to the center of the Earth, and now firectly up to the heavens.

"Motes?" Sarah's voice came from a distance, from all the way down there with her feet planted on the ground, from where she was anchored.

"Maybe it did," she hollered. She imagined the way her voice must have Dopplered past her therapist with each arc of the swing and started to giggle. "Maybe me talking about this with Dry Grass did lead to the letter. Maybe it is my fault."

"You mean you think she went and told Hammered Silver to let her visit you after you talked about your worries?" Sarah called out to her.

"Yeah!"

"What does that change?"

"Nothing!" Motes said, laughing joyously. "It changes nothing. In fact, I hope that *is* the case! At that point, Hammered Silver really *is* just a bitch."

Sarah laughed, and Motes felt the sound in the air as she breezed past, felt her flower crown flutter away in the wind of her passage and fall to the ground in a lazy shower of dandelions, felt the little pink cocktail umbrella A Finger Pointing had tucked behind her ear, by her ma, tug this way and that on her hair.

*I respect her as a person, but I do not like her,* Dry Grass had said. *And I certainly do not respect her authority.*

*Do not worry, my dear,* Dry Grass had said. *You are stuck with me for a good while yet.*

*I would rather tell Hammered Silver to go fuck herself,* Dry Grass had said in the end.

Perhaps Dry Grass had excused herself from the sixth stanza. Perhaps she had taken an opportunity to make her opinions known. Perhaps she had spoken up, talked back, shot down a little bit of Hammered Silver's authority by standing up for Motes.

Perhaps she ought to hug Dry Grass extra-tight next time she saw her.

# 10

Motes played.

She played in the dark. She played crawling on hands and knees. She played hide and seek. She played stealth missions. She played silently, muffling the sound of her passage and keeping her breathing quiet; it was against the rules to turn it off. She played base commander, repelling invisible foes, hollering out orders to her friends. She played noisily, her voice echoing off the rocky walls with laughter and shouts bouncing around seemingly endlessly.

She played in Rock Park, a hulking mound of salmon, pink, gold, and buff flagstone that had been stacked in such a way as to create a series of twisty, narrow tunnels throughout. The tunnels turned sharply, or required her to climb up vague suggestions of ladders made by protruding slabs of rock, or dumped her down into a central cavern, the ground covered in a layer of velvety soft mulch to cushion any falls. The cavern opened out on one end into a broader playground, all of the equipment themed to be related to a quarry: dump trucks and bucket hoists and front end loaders and excavators.

She played throughout the rest of the park, hauling that mulch or digging into it with the equipment or her paws, putting those digger claws of hers to use. She played in the grass, played in the little stands of pine trees that dotted the field beyond, the two whitewashed gazebos. Sometimes there were roller-blades or bikes or skateboards. Sometimes there were self-propelled levitation boots that let you putter along at a few miles per hour a hand's breadth above the ground and which would do all they could to keep you from falling over.

She played with her friends. She played with strangers she had seen before yet never talked to. She played with those she saw once and then never saw again.

She played until she got tired, until enough of her friends got bored and wandered off, until the long, breezy morning in this sim sighed its way into the heat of afternoon. She played until the obvious thing to do was to climb up to the top of the tunnel-ridden pile of flagstone to sit at the summit, enjoying the sun with Alexei.

The park was only one part of a small town, only one part of a sizeable sim, but it was a popular destination for those who leaned into childhood on Lagrange for its permissive attitudes and curious inhabitants, most of whom seemed to be families—found or blood—and many of whom were the kids who played here. Alexei lived here with the family he had built: three guardians—one of whom was his great-grandfather by blood—and a sister.

"I'm glad you're here, Motes," he said after they had sat in silence for some time. "Where were you, anyway? I know you said you didn't want to talk about it, but it's just us, right?"

She shrugged and picked at the rock with a claw, worrying loose a thin chip of flagstone. "I still do not *want* to talk about

it," she said, then grinned over at him. "But I will anyway."

"That's because you never shut up."

She laughed and threw the chip of rock at him. "That is not *not* true. I guess it is extra true, actually, since most of my time away was spent talking." She tried to scratch up another chip, but she seemed to have lucked out that first time. "Sorry I just disappeared a while back."

"Yeah, I was worried. I thought you got hurt real bad. What happened?"

She hesitated, averting her gaze to look out into the park around her, the park she had claimed as her domain not half an hour before. "I got a high priority ping that made me fall, and then I hit my face on that stupid dome."

"I saw you had a bloody nose, yeah," he said, patting her shoulder. "That sucks. Was it a come-home ping?"

"Nah, it was just a warning," she said, speaking slowly while she organized her thoughts, trying to figure out just how much to say. "It was one of my cocladists being rude. She sent me a horrible letter, and wanted me to be in all the wrong moods when I read it, I think."

"Ew."

"Ew is right. She is one of those in the clade that does not like me doing this," she said, gesturing down at herself, out at the playground. "She sent me a huge letter telling me that in a million different ways."

Alexei screwed up his face in a wince. "Double-ew. So were you in trouble? Are you still?"

"I do not think so. At least, everyone is telling me I am not, that it was just her being a b-word and that she just wanted me and my family to feel bad so that she could feel like she had done something."

"So a bully," he said flatly.

Motes giggled. "I mean, I guess so. Big Motes understands it better, but she is busy."

This had long ago become a hint to drop into conversations that to continue would be to break the illusion, to pull back the curtain and expose the play for what it was: merely a performance.

Neither of them, neither of these two consummate performers, wanted that. Alexei could probably pry it out of her, pry out all of the details of all that had happened, pry her out of this space for a little bit if he wanted—and she may yet send him a letter as Big Motes for more context later.

He did not, so he said nothing and flopped backwards on the rock, resting his head on one arm while draping the other over his face to block out the sun. "Sounds dumb," he said. "I'm just glad you're back and that you're not in trouble or anything."

Panting, Motes scooted so that her back rested against a spire of rock to get as much shade as she could. Black fur and bright sun coexisted too energetically at times. "No, not really in trouble," she said. "I may have made myself feel like I was in trouble, but that is just me being a dummy."

There was a snort of laughter from the boy. "That's *definitely* a you thing."

She mulled over this, tallying up the various anxieties she had felt over the years, the worries she had expressed or let color her actions, all the times she disappeared from youth, from play, from this form. Despite her desire to let Big Motes handle such things, a question began to gnaw at her, a desire for feedback. "Yeah, I guess," she mumbled. "You ever get anxious about all this?"

"All this?"

"Being a kid, that sort of thing."

"Isn't this stuff for Big Motes?"

She frowned. "I know, but I want to know. I just got back from two weeks of freaking out."

"Two and a half," Alexei said.

"Please?"

"Hmph."

"Pretty pleeease?" she whined. "With a cherry on top?"

It was his turn to mull things over, apparently, given the comfortable, thoughtful silence that followed. "I dunno. Sometimes, I guess. Sometimes I worry about where I can go like this, right? Like, we met when we were big. We met at that crazy bar with all the crazy music. I go to that stuff as Big Alexei, kinda because I don't want to get trampled, and kinda because I'm worried they'll kick me out."

"Yeah," she said, lining a few pebbles up in a row. "I have been kicked out of lots and lots and lots of places."

"You're also older than I am," he retorted. "So we've probably been kicked out of places at the same rate."

She blew a raspberry at him, got one in return.

"You're not really talking about anxiety, though, right? Like, you're talking about shame, I think."

Another few pebbles wound up in the row as she sat in silence.

"Yeah." He rolled onto his side to look at her, leaving his arm half-draped over his face to block out the sun. "I guess I kinda do, though it always comes from the outside. Like, getting kicked out of a place is whatever, but when someone I meet as Big Alexei learns about Little Alexei and gets all upset and yells at me or cuts contact–"

At this, Motes winced.

He frowned. "That's what happened, isn't it? You had someone cut contact because they learned of it? One of your co-cladists?"

"Yeah," she mumbled. "She already knew, though. She just found out one of her up-trees was still talking to me."

"She made her own up-trees cut contact, too?" He furrowed his brow. "Aren't you guys like super-dispersionistas?"

She laughed. "Some of us. Some of us drifted apart, but some of us stick together really tightly. I have Ma and Bee and a bunch of siblings, right?"

"I guess, yeah," he said. "I'm not a dispersionista, though, so I can't really understand. I don't have any up-trees or cross-trees or whatever. It sucks that she's being a bully, though, 'cause she kind of *is* you, isn't she?"

Motes sighed. "Sort of, yeah. That is why it hurt and why I had to spend a lot of time thinking about it."

He reached out and gave her tail a light tug—not something she usually tolerated, but the conversation had been so gentle that it had no scent of meanness to it—and smiled up to her. "Well, *I* think you're better than she is, so clearly she isn't you. Tell her to get stuffed!"

She laughed, reaching out to bat at his hand. "I guess I pretty much did, because here I am~"

After that, their conversation fell back into more comfortable things. They spoke of friends. They spoke of the pros and cons of Rock Park. They spoke of families and the secret pleasures of being punished. Then they played a half-hearted game of tag before Motes finally said goodbye and stepped home just in time for the evening's planned activities, floating on a cloud of joy like she had not experienced in more than two weeks.

At home, she dashed to the kitchen and gulped down a glass of water, laughed at the uncomfortable chill this left her with, and then ran out into the fading afternoon.

It was a night for good food and terrible movies.

Beholden grilled hot dogs and bratwurst, and Motes, yes, had them loaded up with veggies, dragged through the garden.

Ioan grilled *frigărui*, kebabs loaded up with Carpathian seasonings, and *mititei*, yet another sausage.

Warmth made an array of its best guesses at Artemisian food, some of which were quite tasty. Few who tried the fluffy tower of *frahabrodåt* went back for seconds, at which ey seemed quite proud.

Motes ate it all. She ate herself overfull. She ate herself messy, leaving her shirt dotted with mustard and grease, her lips shining with the oily sheen of at least three different types of sausage.

Thus sated, she darted around the gathering, the thirty or so people who had showed up from both within the clade and without. She hugged everyone who wanted a hug, chased Warmth in multiples, the two little skunks leapfrogging each other and leaving their fur and clothes stained green with with grass. She drank a few margaritas, allowing through only a modicum of the drunkenness so that she remained cognizant and present through the tipsiness, awake and alert through the haze.

She wove around A Finger Pointing and Beholden, drawing figure eights around these anchors of her life with wanderings of herself, trailing love and affection as she went, demanding that they dote upon her, that they lean down so that she could give them nose-dot kisses.

And then, as she had several times over the last week, she latched herself onto Dry Grass. As they had over the last week, they revelled in the closeness and affection, the joy in allowing themselves to be around each other despite meaningless admonitions. As they had, they spoke mostly of small things, of interesting things they had seen or nice foods that they had eaten or simple stories made up on the spot.

It was important to her that she be around this person she considered a member of her family, her Ma 2.0. One of the close ones, not one of the distant ones, not one that had cut her off. One of the ones who reminded her that she was *not* an outcast. It was important that they spend quality time together, that through that time, she *lived* her gratefulness for Dry Grass's presence.

And then, when they all piled into the movie-theater-*cum*-cuddlepit, A Finger Pointing, Beholden, and Dry Grass slouched into a beanbag. Dry Grass dragged Motes into her lap while they all settled in. They sat silent through the first part of movie, watching off and on, dozing now and then. The movie was not important. It was good, she was sure, or bad, but that was not the point.

An hour or so later, after Beholden and A Finger Pointing had well and truly fallen asleep against each other amid all the softness, Dry Grass set up a cone of silence over herself and the skunk, nudged Motes to sit beside her rather than on her, and said, "Hey, kiddo. I would like to apologize for everything that happened this month."

Motes scrubbed her paws over her face to wake up more fully. "How do you mean?"

"All of that wretched business with my down-tree."

"That was not your fault, though. She is just a bit– she is just a b-word."

Dry Grass smiled faintly. "I will let that slide. She is *definitely* a bitch, yes." A pause, and then she continued, "But it rather was my fault, my dear. I mentioned that I had been visiting after that evening with the salad and maccy chee. I made her mad, then told her to go fuck herself."

Motes sat for a moment in silence, watching the movie, half-listening at the muffled audio that made its way through the cone of silence. "I had guessed, yeah."

Her cocladist frowned. "That is why I am sorry. So much happened, and I started it without really thinking of how it would impact everyone."

She shrugged. "But then, maybe I started by whining at you about it. It is nobody's fault but Hammered Silver's." She giggled sleepily, adding, "She made herself mad, even. I do not believe you that you say you did."

Dry Grass's expression softened and she brushed some of the skunk's mane out of her face. "I suppose there is that," she said quietly. "We could go back and forth placing blame as much as we would like–"

"And she would always be the wrong one," Motes interrupted. "Frick her. She is the one holding grudges, we are the ones doing what we want. She is the one hurting people, we are the ones just having fun and playing. She is just a bully. "

There was another moment of silence, of Dry Grass furrowing her brow and thinking, and then at last she lay back on the beanbag and tugged Motes back up to lay on her front. "Yes," she murmured as the skunk got comfortable. "Yes, I guess both of those are true."

They stayed like that for the rest of the film, Dry Grass petting Motes and Motes telling Dry Grass stories about the day, little nothings that showed that fun, that lack of pain.

And then, when the movie was over and many of those in the community center had started to doze on their beanbags and couches, when her ma and Bee put kisses on her snout and left arm in arm, when Dry Grass fell asleep one too many times and begged off to walk back home—not without yet another tight hug from Motes and a promise to be back soon—when Motes caught herself nodding off, she disentangled herself from the rest of that dozy comfort and slipped out into the cool of the night.

Rather than turning left, off toward home, she turned right to the other arm of the 'U' that made up the neighborhood and started wandering through the grass until she hit sidewalk. There, vines in chalk blossomed lazily behind her footsteps, and in the night, in the light of the stars and the moon and the streetlamps, they seemed to glow in pale oranges and whites and blues. She played with them by taking wobbling, drunken steps, crossing one leg in front of the other, pirouetting clumsily to make them tie themselves into knots.

Even so, she continued down around the slow curve of the neighborhood's main street, not bothering to venture into any of the cul-de-sacs. The chalk lines were fun, a little trail describing where the little skunk had wandered, but she *was* tired. It had been a long first day back as Little Motes, and she had successfully packed it to the brim with all that she had wanted to do, and that success gave to her a sense of rightness.

It was a rightness of form—of species, of size, of appearance.

It was a rightness of mindset—of play, of childlike wonder.

It was a recognition of who she was and who she had been and who she could become.

She made it halfway around the bend, down to the very base of the 'U', and, following some whim, some spark of desire, darted back into the grass to race up the ladder of the jungle gym and launch herself down the slide with a shout. She tumbled off the end and into the gravel in an undignified, giggling heap.

Motes played, because how could she not?

# Afterword

# Appendix I — Thoughts on Motes

*Motes Played* was written in a few short weeks at the end of December, 2023 and the beginning of January, 2024 in a burst of creativity. The origin for the story actually stems from a conversation that I had with my partner[1] on a drive from visiting eir parents down in Vancouver back home to northern Washington. In the span of about four hours, we made our way down through the stanzas of the Ode clade and spoke about what make them tick.

There are some known quantities. True Name is the politician, A Finger Pointing is the theatrician, Praiseworthy is the propagandist turned arts administrator, and so on. All of the stanzas have been labeled with their basic ideas, of course, and one of those was Hammered Silver being the center of all of Michelle's feelings on motherhood.

What exactly does that mean, though? How does that play out in her head and her heart?

Our initial take on it was actually fairly negative. We decided that she had some very prescriptive ways of thinking about motherhood. There is caring, yes, but there are also Ways in

---

[1]Whose system name is The Lament, which you may recognize from the dedication.

Which the World Works. After all, Hammered Silver is one of the two who cut her entire stanza off from the eighth and part of the ninth stanzas, as well the Bălan clade, when Sasha worked to reclaim a more fulfilling sense of identity. Later on, this also included the first and then, once they took on Sasha as a stage manager, the fifth stanza.

However, we wanted to toy with those feelings of motherhood more directly. How does she deal with the lack of children on the System? How does she deal with her own feelings on motherhood? We decided on coming up with a good side and a bad side:

- **Good side:** Hammered Silver is keenly focused on family dynamics as a whole and ensuring that these remain supportive in a place where they might otherwise be neglected. This was expanded after the advent of AVEC, where she campaigned to help keep families united after a member uploaded.
- **Bad side:** This problem was expanded vertically to include a very prescriptive definition of family, as she bought thoroughly into the taboo on intraclade relationships. This led her to view *all* family dynamics within clades with distrust and anger.

Well, we already know that there are intraclade relationships sys-side. There always have been, of course, though not always out in public. There have even been intraclade relationships within the Ode clade (and beyond just the stated examples in the Cycle), such as between Beholden and A Finger Pointing.

Not only that, but there were already family dynamics in the clade, with Motes treating A Finger Pointing and Beholden as her parents, Slow Hours as her sister, A Finger Curled and Beholden To The Music Of The Spheres (two long-lived up-trees of A Finger Pointing and Beholden) as her weird gay aunts, and Dry Grass as Ma 2.0.

Boom, automatic conflict.

I wrote in a flurry with The Lament's help, finishing a chapter a day most days over a two week span, working at a similar speed to how *Toledot* came into being. Hypomania be like~[2]

Editing took a bit longer, mind, but was still a nice process, thanks to em, as ey read each chapter aloud to me, refined the story, and wrote portions of the text. Given how much the story means to em as well, it was a joy for both of us. I also got a few beta reads from within the Post-Self community which were, for the most part, really kind and understanding.

The last step on my end was typesetting and final editing pass (which I usually do on the typeset book), getting ready for publication, and getting a cover. I have known Astolpho in some capacity for a few years, though I had been a fan of his art for far longer. We connected in early 2024 and he was quite interested in helping this project come to fruition, so it was lovely to work together.

## The story

I knew that the response to *Motes Played* would be complicated from before its inception. Its inception was bound up in that

---

[2] Okay, but having sciatica for two months probably helped.

very complication. That complication is part and parcel of the book, after all: Motes is an adult—as everyone is, sys-side—and many around her would prefer that she look and act like it.

I knew that the response would be complicated, that it would make readers uncomfortable, would make friends or loved ones have some big feelings. I had those big feelings, too. Even after writing the book, after typesetting it and building the ebook (admittedly a mostly automated process), I struggled with the fact that I had written this thing and was thinking about putting it in front of others. There are no works of mine that are not expressions of vulnerability, but each is vulnerable in its own way. *I* was uncomfortable! Funding it with the *Marsh* Kickstarter was a way to force the issue for myself, to pit my pride in what I had accomplished against my fears.

So anyway, I hit publish.

## Okay, but why a kid?

There are a few reasons why I wrote this book. First and foremost is simply that it was fun. I love the approach that a lot of children's books take with language. All of that repetition lends an almost hypnotic air. You keep reading the same idea over and over being stated in different ways with different antecedents and each one adds a little bit more color to the situation. They slowly change the mood of whatever they are building toward. It is alluring as a writer.

It was also fun to play around with all of the differences that spring up through cladistics. We know Dear is the best worst fox and May Then My Name is a cuddlebug and True Name is a politician and E.W. is a Sad Boi, but if we start prowling through the other stanzas, what do we find?

Well, we know that A Finger Pointing is a theatrician. She is one of the administrators of Au Lieu Du Rêve, the little troupe she started in the early days of the System, but which has grown to a group several hundred strong. This speaks to all sorts of roles that one might pick up, some of them informed by their names and some not. Beholden gets to deal with all of the sound and music, If I Stand Still deals with lights, and Motes gets sets and props

It goes beyond interests or chosen profession (or, well, "profession"; this *is* the System, after all). Years bring with them individuation, and each of these cladists begin to shift as well. Just as May Then My Name is not True Name, neither is Motes A Finger Pointing. A lot can change over time.

This includes all sorts of different aspects of personality. A Finger Pointing remains her flamboyant, dramatic self just as Motes leans hard into these feelings of childhood. I wanted to explore something like this in more detail.

Finally, I have been fascinated with the idea of childhood for years. It is not the supposed purity[3] of it, nor is it necessarily that my own was bad. What it *was*, though, is less than ideal. It feels like my childhood is something that happened to someone else. It is a thing that happened to Matthew, not to Madison. I

---

[3] I find 'the purity of childhood' personally unnerving. It strikes me as an aspect of the oft-maligned purity culture. Kids can be mean. They can be *cruel*. They are creatures who act upon their base desires, for better or worse. I think this, in combination with its laws-for-thee-none-for-me attitude, has led to the "corruption of children" becoming a talking point of the right, those bastions of that very same purity culture.

never got to live a childhood as Madison, good *or* bad.

Honestly, I have little desire to do so now. It is not out of a desire to be a literal kid, myself, that I wrote *Motes Played.* I wrote it because that idea in particular—that someone would wish to just...go be a kid because they can and because it felt good—is fascinating to me. Motes decided that her role was to be the kid, the One Who Plays, and so she leaned hard into that.

I wanted to play with the whole idea, too: I wanted to play with the sorts of uncomfortable feelings that many experience when confronted with adults engaging with the world as children. I wanted to talk about how someone who spends so much time in little space deals with the fact that others hate her guts for it.

## Now, about those big feelings...

I do not need to wonder whether the reaction to *Motes Played* will involve big feelings from others. I have already run into such, both within the Post-Self community spaces and among my broader friends group. At the risk of coming off as defensive, I would like to speak to those feelings.

First, one must consider the role of art. There are three general ways of interpreting art:

- **Escapist:** art is simply there to entertain. In the case of something like fiction, it is there to provide a glimpse of some world other than ours (no matter how distant) so that we can experience something other than our wretched, wretched lives.

- **Representative:** art exists to represent the world as it is. Even things such as science fiction and fantasy represent the tropes that exist within our world, and are used to represent them out of their more complicated context that they might be observed.
- **Instructive:** art should be used to instruct the audience how to interact with the world. This goes beyond simply teaching them how to do this or that, too: it can be that a piece of art is intended to be an example that one should follow.

These are not hard and fast categories, of course, and a work of art need not fill only one of them. I think it is this last one that a lot of folks get hung up on, in cases like this. It is, of course, only a gesture that I provide my intentions in an artist's statement, but there is very little about the book that is intended to be instructive: it starts as children's books do because Motes presents as a kid, and it ends as children's books do because, hey presto, Motes presents as a kid.

Instead, I provide a piece of writing which I intend to be escapist—I have mentioned the joys above—as well as representative. There are littles in the world. It is just a fact! People of all sorts engage with ageplay in all sorts of different ways. If Post-Self is to be a complete take on a future world, then I do not see why it should not include (thoughtful, sensitive, appropriate) takes on complete aspects of the world.

But even if it were instructive, what are the lessons to be taken away from the story?

- **Do not trust strangers not to be gross to kids.** Motes is wary of forming friendships with adults unless she already knows and trusts them. Often, when she does go out as an adult and engages with sexuality, she will not even give her name.

- **Have a support network to help with the first point.** She relies on others not herself to help spot the things that she misses. Those she keeps close—A Finger Pointing, Beholden, Slow Hours, and so on—all strive to protect her, and she trusts in that.
- **Live joyfully but live intentionally.** Motes does not simply throw herself with abandon into "oh, I am going to be a kid now!" but instead approaches her goal with intentionality, setting and respecting boundaries, and choosing spaces where such is expected and welcomed.

And here, of course, are the lessons that it emphatically does *not* teach:

- **It is somehow, in some bizarro universe, okay to groom children, even if those children are adults.** Motes explicitly avoids this and trusts others to help spot the instances she cannot see.

Usually, I am stuck on the number three being used to prove points—hendiatris, bay-*bee*—but I am not going to bother including two more points, because I suspect this will be the only one raised as a concern, even at the expense of any other characterizations presented within the book. After all, Motes also has a death kink that one of her caregivers loathes. She drinks even when presenting as a child. Beholden is an alcoholic and has destructive tantrums, lashing out at those around her. Hammered Silver is a PTA-mom-lookin', HOA-president-ass bitch[4] who abuses her not-husband, Waking World, and Waking World enables a lot of her bullshit.

I do not like the thought that this one sticking point will doubtless lead to strife. I do not like that it will get in the way of people's enjoyment of the work. It is not my responsibility to somehow force readers to enjoy my writing. My responsibility as an author is to present the story.

It is my *desire*, however, to explain where I am coming from.

## Where these feelings come from

If I am coming across as anxious, defensive, or even bitter, I guess it is because, to an extent, I am. I am trying to get better at not apologizing for everything, despite my people-pleasing tendencies. I will tamp down that urge in favor of explaining the roots of these feelings.

I began this essay by talking about my initial wariness at the idea of publishing this thing that I wrote. Since then, I have been struck with the occasional flash of such discomfort, but more and more often, I have been struck with a sense of pride. I *like* what I have accomplished. I like that I wrote in this vaguely children's book style. I like that we get Odists interacting with Odists, and that even the narration is written in (admittedly somewhat gentled) Odespeak. I like that I had the chance to lean into not only my own plurality but The Lament's as well. I like that I got to explore the more populous areas of the System

---

[4]I am contractually obligated to make fun of her. It is part of being an author.

through someone other than the relatively shut-in Bălans. I like that I had the chance to lean into this topic, even! It is fulfilling to write something emotional and difficult.

I remain anxious, I still struggle against defensiveness, and yes, I suppose I do feel a little bitter even still. These are a class of feelings that I try to keep to myself as I work through them. That bitterness, especially, is a reactionary feeling that speaks to complicated thoughts in need of processing, and this contrast between pride in my work and all those big feelings is, yes, plenty complicated.

If I sound at all bitter, then, it is because I have made something that I am proud of and yet also feel compelled to defend, and I resent that.

I resent that I need to be rightfully anxious. I resent that, by creating something in this idea-space, I run the very real risk of, at worst, having my personhood negated when I am declared problematic, a groomer, a pedophile, *persona non grata*. I resent that I do not need to consider whether I will be labeled these things; I am all but sure I will. I mentioned above that I have already had a conversation that touched on this. It led to someone reducing their engagement with the Post-Self community for a while.[5] I resent that I risk losing readers, friends, loved ones. I resent that the oft-misused "death of the author" is only applied to the works one enjoys and derided otherwise, and so in this case, I will be reduced to my roughest edges and discarded by those who do not enjoy works such as these. The work that I

---

[5]Which is valid! Curate your engagement. Stay healthy with your media consumption. The Post-Self community explicitly welcomes a come-and-go, curation-friendly approach in all our spaces.

put into it will be ignored in the face of this one fact regardless of my feelings on what I have accomplished.

I resent that, if I claim that Motes is nearly 300 years old at the time of this story, I will be accused of trying to weasel my way out of grooming accusations, regardless of the fact that dealing with grooming is part of her character and the plot. I resent that if I claim that the headmate upon which Motes is based is actually 38 at time of writing, just like this wretched body,[6] and has simply leaned into feelings of kidcore, a portion of my identity will be declared wicked and manipulative. I resent that, no matter how loudly I say that I am aware of the broader context of CSA in the wider world, how abhorrent I think that is, none of that will matter in the face of that same imagined wicked and manipulative aspect. I resent that, no matter how nuanced my arguments on consent are[7]—even within this very work!—the work itself will be declared, yes, wicked and manipulative.

I resent that one way I could avoid such readings are to make Motes miserable, to deny her happiness in her identity, to take from her her pride in herself and her growth. I resent that I might well be lauded for changing the ending of the book to have Motes give up, have her follow Hammered Silver's suggestion to put away childish things[8] and become other than she had been. I resent that a 'solution' in my straw-reader's mind would be to replace joy with shame.

---

[6]Remember that mention of sciatica? Yeeeah...

[7]Many of those who *do* engage with interests and kinks often considered problematic think about consent and those potentially problematic aspects *far* more than most, even those who dislike them, I guarantee you.

[8]The Odists are famously Jews; why is she quoting 1 Corinthians? But then, I suppose Paul was famously a Jew, too...

It is, as Motes puts it, annihilation. It is the opposite of reclamation. Rather than taking the bad and finding a way to reclaim the good in it, it is taking a thing that is good and making it not just bad, but reprehensible. It is taking things that one enjoys and not making them less enjoyable, but making them shameful.

I resent that.

If I sound bitter, it is because I am proud of what I have made, and I want to share it.

## That aside...

I remain very proud of *Motes Played.* The story was fun to write, the characters were fun to write (and super meaningful besides; thanks plurality!), the responses were fun to hear, and I really hope that the book itself is received well.

It is my hope that this work is enjoyed as a work of escapism. I hope that a work that interrogates little-space and its role in the lives of those who engage with it all plopped into a sci-fi setting leads to readers interrogating the world around them. I hope that, if it is at all instructive, it is instructive on the joys of identity, the hedonism of ever becoming more accurately oneself.

I have come to love Motes, and I hope you do too.

*— Madison Rye Progress*
*April 29, 2024*

# Appendix II — Primer

Post-Self is a science fiction setting involving uploaded consciousnesses and all of the daily dramas that go into their everlasting lives.

This primer is broken into two parts:

- Information on the setting (below), much of which was taken from the Post-Self Wiki.
- Information on the story leading up to *Motes Played* (page 215).

## The setting

Starting in 2115, advances in technology allowed individuals to be uploaded. This is a one-way, destructive procedure. That is, once you are uploaded, there is no going back, and your body dies in the process. Given the ongoing deterioration of the climate on Earth and the fact that, in most countries, uploading is subsidized (one's beneficiaries are provided with a payout after one uploads), this is often seen as a very attractive solution. Other reasons that one might upload is to enjoy the anarchic society on the (deliberately opaquely named) System, the functional immortality offered to uploaded individuals, or some of the mechanics enjoyed by cladists. These cladists live embedded in a giant computer at the center of a space station at the Earth-Moon $L_5$ point known as Lagrange. There are two smaller versions of the System, Castor and Pollux, which were launched in opposite directions traveling out of the Solar System in 2325.

## Cladists

Individuals on the System are known as cladists. This stems from the fact that individuals can create copies of themselves, and those copies can go on to create copies of themselves, and so on. This leads to a branching tree of individuals, or a clade.

'Cladist' refers to both the original upload and any of their numerous copies, and debates about whether or not cladists are still human are a perennial activity.

## Forking, quitting, and merging

The act of a cladist creating a copy of themself is called 'forking', as in a fork in the road or forking a source code repository. This new copy is a complete person. They have their own will and drive to continue living and everything. This is not a hive mind thing: both the original and the copy are true individuals.

That said, this new copy (often called a 'fork' or an 'instance') is, at the moment of forking, the same as the original cladist (called the down-tree instance, because they are closer to the root). After all, that cladist was one person, right? They are just now two! That means that they are created thinking the same sorts of things and sharing the same ideals. Over time, however, they all start to individuate, learning to appreciate their own things based on the separate experiences that they have.

These new instances of our example cladist also have the ability to quit. This means that they all simply stop existing. But wait! Why would they do that?

One reason is that one might simply want to accomplish a task. Perhaps you are cooking a lovely meal and the pasta needs stirring while you are cutting up the garlic bread. Why, simply fork and now you have two pairs of hands, one to go stir the pasta, one to cut the bread. The pasta thus stirred, the new instance may as well just quit. No reason to stick around.

Another reason is to go and experience other things in the world and then bring back those memories. Quite literally, too! When a fork quits, the cladist who forked them receives all of their memories to incorporate with their own. A cladist may wish to cook their delicious meal, but they are also entertaining guests: they can fork off an instance to go cook the meal while they entertain and, when they are done, quit. The down-tree instance will receive all of the memories of having cooked and all of the feelings about the process so that they know to warn their guests, "Hey, uh...the pasta is a liiiittle spicy..."

One can only ever merge down to the one from whom one was forked up until 277+42, and after that point, one can merge to any of one's cocladists, but only within a clade.

"But what about the transporter paradox?" you ask. Post-Self's answer to that is a shrug. The memories live on. All of the experiences live on. One simply lived two lives at once for that time.

## A note on those memories...

One unforeseen consequence of living in a giant computer is the inability to forget. This can start to cause problems as one gets older. And older and older and older...because one is functionally immortal. Even though those memories can be organized, or even storied away in imaginary bins called exocortices to be remembered on demand, the fact that they keep piling up is both a boon and a bane. It is a boon because now, suddenly, you can remember everything! No more forgetting names, no more losing track of items. It is a bane, though, because that can get kind of maddening for your average 300 year old.

## Creating

For instance, they can create just about anything they can dream up. This is not as easy as it sounds, of course; it takes skill to get good at dreaming up very specific things such as strawberries or cars or a pencil.

They can also create sims. These are the locations where they live out their lives. These can be everything from a studio apartment to an entire city. They can be private or public. They can be ornate and finely detailed natural settings or they can be plain gray cubes of space.

## Crashing and CPV

Occasionally, something will happen and a cladist will crash. This is usually not too big of a deal, as it can be sorted out by a systech and the cladist brought back to life.

Contraproprioceptive virus is the only way to kill a cladist. It disrupts their sense of their body and induces a crash, from which one cannot recover. This was patched out in 2401 — alas, that is still a few decades off from this story.

## Sensoria

Cladists engage with the world with all of the same senses that we have. These are lumped together into a sensorium. One of the benefits they have is the ability to share some or all of these senses with another cladist as a form of co-experiencing via a sensorium linkage, or as a tool in the form of a sensorium message. If you want to show your friend what you are looking at, send them a sensorium message to share your vision. Some sims even mess with your sensoria (consensually, of course) to change the way that you see things or how things feel.

## The perisystem architecture

There are some tools included in the System itself in what is called the perisystem architecture.

All of those creations listed above, and even some of these experiences, can be shared publicly on the exchange. This was originally a marketplace where one bought and sold such things with Reputation, a currency put in place in the early days when System capacity needed closer management, though this has since become almost a non-issue.

There are also feeds which one can use to share information, news, stories, all sorts of things! Think of these (loosely) like sub-reddits.

The perisystem also contains the clade listing. Privacy was an important consideration from the founding of the System, so one cannot simply look up any old cladist and find out everything about them without being granted permission.

Finally, it just plain stores information. Things like libraries are essentially locations to go engage with, access, manipulate, or otherwise play with the information that is always available.

# The characters

People upload for lots of reasons! Once they are sys-side, though, they settle into society as they will.

### It is an anarchy

There is no way to truly govern such a system beyond the mechanics provided by its very existence, and so it is simply left ungoverned. The forces behind the scenes have largely sought only to guide the System in vague directions, often towards yet more freedom. Rules are per-sim, engagement is optional, and cultures are fractured and finely tuned around shared interests or heritage.

### It is queer-normative

The System allows for endless freedom and endless expression. In such a setting, boundaries such as strict gender binaries, hetero- and mono-normative relationship structures, and even species have been broken down. Trans folks may upload and live as they will as cis folks of their chosen gender, or they may remain visibly and proudly trans. Furries may upload and become their fursoñas (this is a metafurry setting, after all; everyone on Earth is a human, and thus every cladist began life as a human). Plural and median systems may upload and split into component selves, or they may remain plural sys-side. Even names and identity have been queered, and you will often see clades adopting naming schemes such as taking lines of a poem for their forks' names.

## Why are there so many skunks?

If you have seen cladists out and about on the web, the chances are good that you have seen some skunks among their number, usually with long, poetic names. This is due largely to the canon works in the Post-Self cycle which feature anthropomorphic skunks heavily. Several folks have adopted these skunks as headmates or characters for roleplaying.

✬

## The story so far

The story leading up to *Motes Played* is told in the four books of the Post-Self Cycle: *Qoheleth*, *Toledot*, *Nevi'im*, and *Mitzvot*. Here, let me spoil them all for you:

### *Qoheleth*

In 2112, RJ Brewster (known to eir friends as AwDae), an audio technician for the Soho Theatre Troupe gets "lost": a virus trips a safeguard in the implants ey uses to connect to the immersive 'net, which locks em within eir own dreams, leaving em in an apparent state of catatonia. In the months leading up to this, several people in the Western Federation have gotten lost, and Dr. Carter Ramirez is tasked with figuring out just how to help them, but she has been encountering more friction than expected in the course of doing her job.

She is joined on her search by Michelle Hadje — who goes by the moniker Sasha in furry spaces — though as they start to realize that the origin of the Lost is not a virus but a way for the government of the Western Fed to disappear undesirables, Sasha, too, is lost. Once Dr. Ramirez manages to break the case wide open and all of the Lost are resuscitated, it is found that none of them remain the same, each having suffered some deep neurological trauma.

In the end, AwDae defects to the Sino-Russian Bloc — the other major world power — to volunteer to be one of the first to upload to a new world.

Nearly two hundred years in the future in 2305, Ioan Bălan is contacted by an enigmatic fennec fox named Dear, Also, The Tree That Was Felled of the Ode clade who needs eir help finding someone and solving a mystery. Someone has revealed a secret — the name of a loved one — which puts its clade at risk. After a journey down several strangely-shaped rabbit holes, they discover that one of the Odists was at the heart of this mystery. Now going by Qoheleth and clearly struggling with delusions of grandeur, he has sent Ioan and the Odists on a wild chase to get them invested in his discovery: memory on the System is eternal, and all of the oldest uploads are at risk of slowly losing touch with reality.

In the midst of explaining this to all of the Ode clade, he is assassinated in grand fashion by one of the other guests — someone who Dear assumes is one of the more conservative Odists.

In the end, it is revealed that the Odists are all descended from Michelle/Sasha, who uploaded in 2117, and that the name they keep secret is that of AwDae, who Dear explains killed emself. In eir final note, ey left Sasha/Michelle with a poem containing the lines from which they take their names.

The version of Ioan who agreed to this adventure, having found emself changed far beyond eir root instance, decides to become eir own cladist, adopting the name Codrin Bălan.

## *Toledot*

In 2325, two smaller versions of the System named Castor and Pollux are launched in opposite directions on a long journey out of the Solar System, leaving the original System, now called Lagrange, behind in orbit around Earth. The date, Ioan realizes, is important due to it being the 200th anniversary of the secession of the System from the governments of Earth, and the correspondences start to pile up from there. Working with another Odist, May Then My Name Die With Me, on Lagrange and Codrin Bălan over on Castor and Pollux ey starts to compile a history of the System from its foundation.

After the trauma of getting lost, Michelle/Sasha uploads as soon as she can afford to. With her experience in campaigning for the Lost, she joins the Council of Eight, a guiding body for the early System, but quickly finds herself overwhelmed, as she struggles to maintain a single identity — either Sasha or Michelle — as well as a single form — either skunk or human.

Promising herself a two week vacation, she forks the first ten members of the Ode clade, each taking the first line from the ten stanzas of AwDae's poem. The vacation turns out to be permanent, and shortly after the events of *Qoheleth*, she summons the rest of the clade to merge down so that she can experience their joys and sorrows, and then quits forever.

The Only Time I Know My True Name Is When I Dream — or just True Name — remains on the Council as the political member of the clade while the other skunks/women/skunkwomen wander off to work on other projects. She is tasked by Jonas, another councilmember, with aiding in the campaign for secession. She finds it surprisingly easy and surprisingly fulfilling, quickly leaning into the role of the politician, using her skills as an actress and theatre teacher to help sway those around her, as well as their phys-side friend, Yared Zerezghi, to accomplish her goal.

After Launch, much of this information comes to light, along with the fact that, despite the Council of Eight being disbanded in the 2150s, Jonas and True Name (along with the rest of the eighth stanza) continue to steer the politics of not just the System but the governments of Earth from behind the scenes — or so they say. So dramatic are their stories, that the Bălans' book, *An Expanded History of Our World*, comes off more as sensationalist schlock than anything serious.

This, it seems, is by design.

In an epilogue in 2346, astronomer Tycho Brahe on the launch vehicle Castor receives a transmission from an outside source: someone has picked up their signal and would like to meet.

## *Nevi'im*

With the signal from the Artemisians, as the aliens are dubbed, True Name and Jonas leap into action to prepare not just for the arrival of the Artemisian emissaries but also to shape the reception of this news for the remainder of Castor — and the other Systems beyond.

Codrin is, of course, tapped to help document and take part in this project along with Tycho Brahe, True Name, Why Ask Questions Here At The End Of All Things, and Sarah Genet, a psychologist. Given the effects that the Bălans' *History* has had, few people seem to trust that True Name's heart is in the right place, despite her assurances otherwise and apparent earnestness.

The Artemisians — actually four different alien races traveling on a single ship, also taking the form of an uploaded-consciousness system — agree to send a delegation of five to Castor to meet with humanity's delegation, while our five intrepid heroes prepare to transfer to Artemis to accomplish two meetings in parallel. Artemis, however, does not have forking. Instead, they have malleable control over time. This is so close to what the Odists experienced while lost that both True Name and Why Ask Questions immediately begin to struggle just as Michelle/Sasha did so many years ago.

Did I say Why Ask Questions? I meant Answers Will Not Help: those sneaky politicians decide to test their luck by sending a subtly different delegation to Artemis than the one on Castor.

Things are not quite so easy back on Lagrange. True Name is struggling, and when she meets up with Ioan and May Then My Name — now disgustingly cute partners — things do not go well. May falls into 'overflow', a sort of rapid mood swing that all Odists seem to experience, and in the process, two of her cocladists quit, leaving the Ode clade now numbering ninety-seven.

While Ioan tries to pick apart what is going on with True Name, ey winds up befriending her, seeing that, no, really, she is just as earnest and vulnerable as eir own partner, and the act that she put on during the writing of the *History* has left her overworked and lonely.

The meetings go about as well as can be expected. That is to say, on Castor, they go fine, and on Artemis, Answers Will Not Help loses her mind and somehow manages to quit, despite such not being possible. At the end of three days and having had their ruse brought to light, the delegates learn that the end goal of this convergence is to establish whether or not humanity will be able to join Artemis on its ongoing travels around the galaxy.

The final step is simply to want to, and when Tycho admits this in a meeting, they are formally welcomed aboard as the fifth race.

The prologue and epilogue detail the story of AwDae leaving behind eir life in London to travel to the S-R Bloc to be a part of an experiment, searching for a way to upload a mind to a computer. All previous attempts have failed, but they have hope that, with the information gained from em getting lost, eirs will be a success. In the end, although ey emself does not wind up within the System, eir mind becomes a part of the foundation, leading to all future successful uploads, which explains while all of the Odists say that they can feel em within.

## *Mitzvot*

Four years after convergence, Ioan is still meeting with True Name on a monthly basis. Nominally meetings to maintain friendly relations between True Name and May Then My Name, these meetings show real friendship between the two. They also show that True Name is struggling more and more over time. On Secession day, 2350, Jonas attempts to assassinate True Name, killing 106 of her forks and leaving the instance who was visiting Ioan the sole living instance of her. Jonas, when confronted by Ioan, demands that True Name meet with em before the end of the year to discuss his plan B — it is that or hide away forever. He requests that Ioan write a book about this to help shape this outcome as he would like.

Forced together as she goes into hiding, True Name and May Then My Name struggle to get along, with mixed results. While they find it easy enough to remain polite, some of the information that True Name shares sets May off; it turns out that, in order to gain leverage over her, Jonas set True Name up with a snarky and dapper fox named Zacharias, a long, *long* diverged fork of May Then My Name's, using the taboo against intraclade relationships as a means of control.

A few days later, in the heat of the moment, May talks one of True Name's other up-tree instances, End Waking, into merging down with her. Given how much End Waking hates her guts, this does not go well for True Name, leaving her feeling torn in two. While May feels quite bad for having hurt her, True Name at least understands her stated goal of helping her become more — or at least other — than what she was.

In an attempt to reconcile, May herself merges down, leaving True Name feeling a more comfortable plurality, though it also leaves her with May's love for Ioan. Her identity is now that of True Name, that of End Waking, and that of May Then My Name.

Jonas calls on her to appear before him in one final meeting, where she seeks a way to remain alive. All of her experience in theatre and politics pays off and she changes both her shape and her name, going now by Sasha. Given the empathetic view that many have of the Sasha/Michelle of old, this means that Jonas cannot do anything to her without putting himself at risk, and she is free (with some restrictions; no going back into politics) to live on.

In an extended epilogue, the book, *Individuation and Reconciliation*, is published and Ioan enters a sometimes-relationship with Sasha, whenever she is feeling up to being around people, given that she now has three different types of overflow, two of which lead to her requesting space from others. She — along with the rest of the eighth stanza, the Bălan clade, and Dear — have been cut off from the sixth and seventh stanzas (those of Hammered Silver and In Dreams) for her actions.

## And so now...

By the time of the story of *Motes Played*, Sasha has started working with Au Lieu Du Rêve (when she is able, at least) as a stage manager. She — along with May and Ioan — have been welcomed into the arms of the fifth stanza (that of A Finger Pointing) with love and kindness. The taboo around intraclade relationships has quickly loosened, and the System has entered once more into a sort of long peace.

✩

Post-Self an open setting, meaning that anyone can create content within it, though the canon is loosely managed in order to keep it consistent. If you enjoyed this story and any of the many others within this universe, it is open for you to write, draw — or paint! — or otherwise create within. For more creative Post-Self endeavors, look no further than *post-self.ink*, and for more information than you could ever want, check out the Post-Self Wiki over at *wiki.post-self.ink*

# Acknowledgments

Thanks, as always, to the polycule, who have been endlessly supportive. Thanks as well as to Tomash, Ellen, Andréa, Faux, and all the rest of the Post-Self community, who have helped build this lovely world, to Isiat and Faux for their kind words, and to Lilium who made me think most about the impact of my work.
— *Madison Rye Progress*

✩

Thanks also to Madison's patrons:

**$10+**  Ammy; Andréa C. Mason; Donna Karr (thanks, mom); Erika Kovac; Fuzz Wolf; green; Kit Redgrave; Merry Cearley; Mx. Juniper System; Orrery; Rob; Sariya Meolody

**$5**  Some Egrets; ramshackle; Christi; Erica; Junkie Dawg; Lhexa; Lorxus, an actual fox on the internet; Norm Steadman; Petrov Neutrino; raxraxraxraxrax; Sasha Moore, Strawberry Daquiri; ubuntor; Zeta Syanthis

**$1**  Alicia Goranson; Ayla Ounce; Bel; BowieBarks; Katt, sky-guided vulpine friend; Kindar; Muruski; Peter Hayes; Ruari ORourke; Sethvir; Yana Winters

Thanks is due as well to all of the backers of the *Marsh* Kickstarter, without whom this paperback edition of *Motes Played* would not be possible:

**Krzysztof Drewniak, Nathan Merrifield, Andréa CERES Mason, Lhexa,** *Strawberry, Amdusias, Saphire Lattice, Ash Holland, Michael Miele, Ashley Hale, Mimir, Vendryth, Petrov Neutrino, Alexandrea Christina Leal,* Kuviare, Nova, Vernon Jones, Andy Oxenreider, LadyLenalia, ramshackle heather, MisfitMephit, Some Egrets, NightEyes DaySpring, critters-system, doctorlit, Rachel Dillon, Joel Kreissman, Kate Eckhart, Giantrobots42, raine, Ayla Ounce, Alicia E. Goranson, James Tatum, Saghiir, Ember Cloke, Payson R. Harris, Vulpis, lenientsy, Campbell Royales, Laura, AntarcticFox, ubuntor, Asha Jade Goodwin, Barac Baker Wiley, Me, Robert Armstrong, Sethvir, Richie

# About the authors

Madison Rye Progress and Samantha Yule Fireheart are a couple'a nerds living in the mountains with their dog. Together, they have shepherded the Post-Self universe from a simple setting for a few stories to an entire world, working to curate the history and mechanics, as well as building the community that has sprung up around the setting.

makyo.ink

everdream.space

# About the artist

B. Root is a illustrator, 3d artist, and VR enthusiast living in the Pacific Northwest. He is also a rather small lion.

roots.works

www.ingramcontent.com/pod-product-compliance
Lightning Source LLC
Chambersburg PA
CBHW051758050726

47598CB00006B/2341